C000011042

Germinal
Volume III

Emile Zola

Copyright Notice

The text in this book has been downloaded from the internet and has been extensively edited and typeset.

Copyright © 2006 Objective Systems Pty Ltd ACN 085 119 953

CONTENTS

Part 6

Chapter 1

THE first fortnight of February passed and a black cold prolonged the hard winter without pity for the poor. Once more the authorities had scoured the roads; the prefect of Lille, an attorney, a general, and the police were not sufficient, the military had come to occupy Montsou; a whole regiment of men were camped between Beaugnies and Marchiennes. Armed pickets guarded the pits, and there were soldiers before every engine. The manager's villa, the Company's Yards, even the houses of certain residents, were bristling with bayonets. Nothing was heard along the streets but the slow movement of patrols. On the pit-bank of the Voreux a sentinel was always placed in the frozen wind that blew up there, like a look-out man above the flat plain; and every two hours, as though in an enemy's country, were heard the sentry's cries:

"Qui vive? – Advance and give the password!"

Nowhere had work been resumed. On the contrary, the strike had spread; Crévecoeur, Mirou, Madeleine, like the Voreux, were producing nothing; at Feutry-Cantel and the Victoire there were fewer men every morning; even at Saint-Thomas, which had been hitherto exempt, men were wanting. There was now a silent persistence in the face of this exhibition of force which exasperated the miners' pride. The settlements looked deserted in the midst of the beetroot fields. Not a workman stirred, only at rare intervals was one to be met by chance, isolated, with sidelong look, lowering his head before the red trousers. And in this deep melancholy calm, in this passive opposition to the guns, there was a deceptive gentleness, a forced and patient obedience of wild beasts in a cage, with their eyes on the tamer, ready to spring on his neck if he turned his back. The Company, who were being ruined by this death of work, talked of hiring miners from the Borinage, on the Belgian frontier, but did not dare; so that the battle continued as before between the colliers, who were shut up at home, and the dead pits guarded by soldiery.

On the morrow of that terrible day this calm had come about at once, hiding such a panic that the greatest silence possible was kept concerning the damage and the atrocities. The inquiry which had been opened showed that Maigrat had died from his fall, and the frightful mutilation of the corpse remained uncertain, already surrounded by a legend. On its side, the Company did not acknowledge the disasters it had suffered, any more than the Grégoires cared to compromise their daughter in the scandal of a trial in which she would have to give evidence. However, some arrests took place, mere supernumeraries as usual, silly and frightened, knowing nothing. By mistake, Pierron was taken off with handcuffs on his wrists as far as Marchiennes, to the great amusement of his mates. Rasseneur, also, was nearly arrested by two gendarmes. The management was content with preparing lists of names and giving back certificates in large numbers. Maheu had received his, Levaque also, as well as thirty-four of their mates in the settlement of the Deux-Cent-Quarante alone. And all the severity was directed against Étienne, who had disappeared on the evening of the fray, and who was being sought, although no trace of him could be found. Chaval, in his hatred, had denounced him, refusing to name the others at Catherine's appeal, for she wished to save her parents. The days passed, every one felt that nothing was yet concluded; and with oppressed hearts every one was awaiting the end.

At Montsou, during this period, the inhabitants awoke with a start every night, their ears buzzing with an imaginary alarmbell and their nostrils haunted by the smell of powder. But what completed their discomfiture was a sermon by the new curé, Abbé Ranvier, that lean priest with eyes like red-hot coals who had succeeded Abbé Joire. He was indeed unlike the smiling discreet man, so fat and gentle, whose only anxiety was to live at peace with everybody. Abbé Ranvier went so far as to defend these abominable brigands who had dishonoured the district. He found excuses for the atrocities of the strikers; he violently attacked the middle class, throwing on them the whole of the responsibility. It was the middle class which, by dispossessing the Church of its ancient liberties in order to misuse them itself, had turned this world into a cursed place of injustice and suffering; it was the middle class which prolonged misunderstandings, which was pushing on towards a terrible catastrophe by its atheism, by its refusal to return to the old beliefs, to the fraternity of the early Christians. And he dared to threaten the rich. He warned them that if they obstinately persisted in refusing to listen to the voice of God, God would surely put Himself on the side of the poor. He would take back their fortunes from those who faithlessly enjoyed them, and would distribute them to the humble of the earth for the triumph of His glory. The devout trembled at this; the lawyer declared that it was Socialism of the worst kind; all saw the cur at the head of a band, brandishing a cross, and with vigorous blows demolishing the bourgeois society of '89.

M. Hennebeau, when informed, contented himself with saying, as he shrugged his shoulders:

"If he troubles us too much the bishop will free us from him."

And while the breath of panic was thus blowing from one end of the plain to the other, Étienne was dwelling beneath the earth, in Jeanlin's burrow at the bottom of Réquillart. It was there that he was in hiding; no one believed him so near; the quiet audacity of that refuge, in the very mine, in that abandoned passage of the old pit, had baffled search. Above, the sloes and hawthorns growing among the fallen scaffolding of the belfry filled up the mouth of the hole. No one ventured down; it was necessary to know the trick – how to hang on to the roots of the mountain ash and to let go fearlessly, to catch hold of the rungs that were still solid. Other obstacles also protected him, the suffocating heat of the passage, a hundred and twenty metres of dangerous descent, then the painful gliding on all fours for a quarter of a league between the narrowed walls of the gallery before discovering the brigand's cave full of plunder. He lived there in the midst of abundance, finding gin there, the rest of the dried cod, and provisions of all sorts. The large hay bed was excellent, and not a current of air could be felt in this equal temperature, as warm as a bath. Light, however, threatened to fail. Jeanlin, who had made himself purveyor, with the prudence and discretion of a savage and delighted to make fun of the police, had even brought him pomatum, but could not succeed in putting his hands on a packet of candles.

After the fifth day Étienne never lighted up except to eat. He could not swallow in the dark. This complete and interminable night, always of the same blackness, was his chief torment. It was in vain that he was able to sleep in safety, that he was warm and provided with bread, the night had never weighed so heavily on his brain. It seemed to him even to crush his thoughts. Now he was living on thefts. In spite of his communistic theories, old scruples of education arose, and he contented himself with gnawing his share of dry bread. But what was to be done? One must live, and his task was not yet accomplished. Another shame overcame him: remorse for that savage drunkenness from the gin, drunk in the great cold on an empty stomach, which had thrown him, armed with a knife, on Chaval. This stirred in him the whole of that unknown terror, the hereditary ill, the long ancestry of drunkenness, no longer tolerating a drop of alcohol without falling into homicidal mania. Would he then end as a murderer? When he found himself in shelter, in this profound calm of the earth, seized by satiety of violence, he had slept for two days the sleep of a brute, gorged and overcome; and the depression continued, he lived in a bruised state with bitter mouth and aching head, as after some tremendous spree. A week passed by; the Maheus, who had been warned, were not able to send a candle; he had to give up the enjoyment of light, even when eating.

Now Étienne remained for hours stretched out on his hay. Vague ideas were working within him for the first time: a feeling of superiority, which placed him apart from his mates, an exaltation of his person as he grew more instructed. Never had he reflected so much; he asked himself the why of his disgust on the morrow of that furious course among the pits; and he did not dare to reply to himself, his recollections were repulsive to him, the ignoble desires, the coarse instincts, the odour of all that wretchedness shaken out to the wind. In spite of the torment of the darkness, he would come to hate the hour for returning to the settlement. How nauseous were all these wretches in a heap, living at the common bucket! There was not one with whom he could seriously talk politics; it was a bestial existence, always the same air tainted by onion, in which one choked! He wished to enlarge their horizon, to raise them to the comfort and good manners of the middle class, by making them masters; but how long it would take! and he no longer felt the courage to await victory, in this prison of hunger. By slow degrees his vanity of leadership, his constant preoccupation of thinking in their place, left him free, breathing into him the soul of one of those bourgeois whom he execrated.

Jeanlin one evening brought a candle-end, stolen from a carter's lantern, and this was a great relief for Étienne. When the darkness began to stupefy him, weighing on his skull almost to madness, he would light up for a moment; then, as soon as he had chased away the nightmare, he extinguished the candle, miserly of this brightness which was as necessary to his life as bread. The silence buzzed in his ears, he only heard the flight of a band of rats, the cracking of the old timber, the tiny sound of a spider weaving her web. And with eyes open, in this warm nothingness, he returned to his fixed idea – the thought of what his mates were doing above. Desertion on his part would have seemed to him the worst cowardice. If he thus hid himself, it was to remain free, to give counsel or to act. His long meditations had fixed his ambition. While awaiting something better he would like to be Pluchart, leaving manual work in order to work only at politics, but alone, in a clean room, under the pretext that brain labour absorbs the entire life and needs quiet.

At the beginning of the second week, the child having told him that the police supposed he had gone over to Belgium, Étienne ventured out of his hole at nightfall. He wished to ascertain the situation, and to decide if it was still well to persist. He himself considered the game doubtful. Before the strike he felt uncertain of the result, and had simply yielded to facts; and now, after having been intoxicated with rebellion, he came back to this first doubt, despairing of making the Company yield. But he would not yet confess this to himself; he was tortured when he thought of the miseries of defeat, and the heavy responsibility of suffering which would weigh upon him. The end of the strike: was it not the end of his part, the overthrow of his ambition, his life falling back into the brutishness of the mine and the horrors of the settlement? And honestly, without any base calculation or falsehood, he endeavoured to find his faith again, to prove to himself that resistance was still possible, that Capital was about to destroy itself in face of the heroic suicide of Labour.

Throughout the entire country, in fact, there was nothing but a long echo of ruin. At night, when he wandered through the black country, like a wolf who has come out of his forest, he seemed to hear the crash of bankruptcies from one end of the plain to the other. He now passed by the roadside nothing but closed dead workshops, becoming rotten beneath the dull sky. The sugar works had especially suffered: the Hoton sugar works, the Fauvelle works, after having reduced the number of their hands, had come to grief one after the other. At the Dutilleul flour works the last mill had stopped on the second Saturday of the month, and the Bleuze rope works, for mine cables, had been quite ruined by the strike. On the Marchiennes side the situation was growing worse every day. All the fires were out the Gagebois glass works, men were continually being sent away from the Sonneville workshops, only one of the three blast furnaces of the Forges was alight, and not one battery of coke ovens was burning on the horizon. The strike of the Montsou colliers, born of the industrial crisis which had been growing worse for two years, had increased it and precipitated the downfall. To the other causes of suffering – the stoppage of orders from America, and the engorgement of invested capital in excessive production – was now added the unforeseen lack of coal for the few furnaces which were still kept up; and that was the supreme agony, this engine bread which the pits no longer furnished. Frightened by the general anxiety, the Company, by diminishing its output and starving its miners, inevitably found itself at the end of December without a fragment of coal at the surface of its pits. Everything held together, the plague blew from afar, one fall led to another; the industries tumbled each other over as they fell, in so rapid a series of catastrophes that the shocks echoed in the midst of the neighbouring cities, Lille,

Douai, Valenciennes, where absconding bankers were bringing ruin on whole families.

At the turn of a road Étienne often stopped in the frozen night to hear the rubbish raining down. He breathed deeply in the darkness, the joy of annihilation seized him, the hope that day would dawn on the extermination of the old world, with not a single fortune left standing, the scythe of equality levelling everything to the ground. But in this massacre it was the Company's pits that especially interested him. He would continue his walk, blinded by the darkness, visiting them one after the other, glad to discover some new disaster. Landslips of increasing gravity continued to occur on account of the prolonged abandonment of the passages. Above the north gallery of Mirou the ground sank in to such an extent, that the Joiselle road, for the distance of a hundred metres, had been swallowed up as though by the shock of an earthquake; and the Company, disturbed at the rumours raised by these accidents, paid the owners for their vanished fields without bargaining. Crévecoeur and Madeleine, which lay in very shifting rock, were becoming stopped up more and more. It was said that two captains had been buried at the Victoire; there was an inundation at Feutry-Cantel, it had been necessary to wall up a gallery for the length of a kilometre at Saint-Thomas, where the ill-kept timbering was breaking down everywhere. Thus every hour enormous sums were spent, making great breaches in the shareholders' dividends; a rapid destruction of the pits was going on, which must end at last by eating up the famous Montsou deniers which had been centupled in a century.

In the face of these repeated blows, hope was again born in Étienne; he came to believe that a third month of resistance would crush the monster – the weary, sated beast, crouching down there like an idol in his unknown tabernacle. He knew that after the Montsou troubles there had been great excitement in the Paris journals, quite a violent controversy between the official newspapers and the opposition newspapers, terrible narratives, which were especially directed against the International, of which the empire was becoming afraid after having first encouraged it; and the directors not daring to turn a deaf ear any longer, two of them had condescended to come and hold an inquiry, but with an air of regret, not appearing to care about the upshot; so disinterested, that in three days they went away again, declaring that everything was going on as well as possible. He was told, however, from other quarters that during their stay these gentlemen sat permanently, displaying feverish activity, and absorbed in transactions of which no one about them uttered a word. And he charged them with affecting confidence they did not feel, and came to look upon their departure as a nervous flight, feeling now certain of triumph since these terrible men were letting everything go.

But on the following night Étienne despaired again. The Company's back was too robust to be so easily broken; they might lose millions, but later on they would get them back again by gnawing at their men's bread. On that night, having pushed as far as Jean-Bart, he guessed the truth when an overseer told him that there was talk of yielding Vandame to Montsou. At Deneulin's house, it was said, the wretchedness was pitiful, the wretchedness of the rich; the father ill in his powerlessness, aged by his anxiety over money, the daughters struggling in the midst of tradesmen, trying to save their shifts. There was less suffering in the famished settlements than in this middle-class house where they shut themselves up to drink water. Work had not been resumed at Jean-Bart, and it had been necessary to replace the pump at Gaston-Marie; while, in spite of all haste, an inundation had already begun which made great expenses necessary. Deneulin had at last risked his request for a loan of one hundred thousand francs from the Grégoires. and the refusal, though he had expected it, completed his ejection: if they refused, it was for his sake, in order to save him from an impossible struggle; and they advised him to sell. He, as usual, violently refused. It enraged him to have to pay the expenses of the strike; he hoped at first to die of it, with the blood at his head, strangled by apoplexy. Then what was to be done? He had listened to the directors' offers. They wrangled with him, they depreciated this superb prey, this repaired pit, equipped anew, where the lack of capital alone paralysed the output. He would be lucky if he got enough out of it to satisfy his creditors. For two days he had struggled against the directors at Montsou, furious at the quiet way with which they took advantage of his embarrassment and shouting his refusals at them in his loud voice. And there the affairs remained, and they had returned to Paris to await patiently his last groans. Étienne smelled out this compensation for the disasters, and was again seized by discouragement before the invincible power of the great capitalists, so strong in battle that they fattened in defeat by eating the corpses of the small capitalists who fell at their side.

The next day, fortunately, Jeanlin brought him a piece of good news. At the Voreux the tubbing of the shaft was threatening to break, and the water was filtering in from all the joints; in great haste a gang of carpenters had been set on to repair it.

Up to now Étienne had avoided the Voreux, warned by the everlasting black silhouette of the sentinel stationed on the pit-bank above the plain. He could not be avoided, he dominated in the air, like the flag of the regiment. Towards three o'clock in the morning the sky became overcast, and he went to the pit, where some mates explained to him the bad condition of the tubbing; they even thought that it would have to be done entirely over again, which would stop the output of coal for three months. For a long time he prowled round, listening to the carpenters' mallets hammering in the shaft. That wound which had to be dressed rejoiced his heart.

As he went back in the early daylight, he saw the sentinel still on the pit-bank. This time he would certainly be seen. As he walked he thought about those soldiers who were taken from the people, to be armed against the people. How easy the triumph of the revolution would be if the army were suddenly to declare for it! It would be enough if the workman and the peasant in the barracks were to remember their origin. That was the supreme peril, the great terror, which made the teeth of the middle class chatter when they thought of a possible defection of the troops. In two hours they would be swept away and exterminated with all the delights and abominations of their iniquitous life. It was already said that whole regiments were tainted with Socialism. Was it true? When justice came, would it be thanks to the cartridges distributed by the middle class? And snatching at another hope, the young man dreamed that the regiment, with its posts, now guarding the pits, would come over to the side of the strikers, shoot down the Company to a man, and at last give the mine to the miners.

He then noticed that he was ascending the pit-bank, his head filled with these reflections. Why should he not talk with this soldier? He would get to know what his ideas were. With an air of indifference, he continued to come nearer, as though he were gleaning old wood among the rubbish. The sentinel remained motionless.

"Eh, mate! damned weather," said Étienne, at last. "I think we shall have snow."

He was a small soldier, very fair, with a pale, gentle face covered with red freckles. He wore his military greatcoat with the awkwardness of a recruit,

"Yes, perhaps we shall, I think," he murmured.

And with his blue eyes he gazed at the livid sky, the smoky dawn, with soot weighing like lead afar over the plain.

"What idiots they are to put you here to freeze!" Étienne went on. "One would think the Cossacks were coming! And then there's always wind here."

The little soldier shivered without complaining. There was certainly a little cabin of dry stones there, where old Bonnemort used to take shelter when it blew a hurricane, but the order being not to leave the summit of the pit-bank, the soldier did not stir from it, his hands so stiffened by cold that he could no longer feel his weapon. He belonged to the guard of sixty men who were protecting the Voreux, and as this cruel sentry-duty frequently came round, he had before nearly stayed there for good with his dead feet. His work demanded it; a passive obedience finished the benumbing process, and he replied to these questions with the stammered words of a sleepy child.

Étienne in vain endeavoured during a quarter of an hour to make him talk about politics. He replied "yes" or "no" without seeming to understand. Some of his comrades said that the captain was a republican; as to him, he had no idea — it was all the same to him. If he was ordered to fire, he would fire, so as not to be punished. The workman listened, seized with the popular hatred against the army – against these brothers whose hearts were changed by sticking a pair of red pantaloons on to their buttocks.

"What's your name?"

"Jules."

"And where do you come from?"

"From Plogof, over there."

He stretched out his arm at random. It was in Brittany, he knew no more. His small pale face grew animated. He began to laugh, and felt warmer.

"I have a mother and a sister. They are waiting for me, sure enough. Ah! it won't be for tomorrow. When I left, they came with me as far as Pont-l'Abbé. We had to take the horse to Lepalmec: it nearly broke its legs at the bottom of the Audierne Hill. Cousin Charles was waiting for us with sausages, but the women were crying too much, and it stuck in our throats. Good Lord! what a long way off our home is!"

His eyes grew moist, though he was still laughing. The desert moorland of Plogof, that wild storm-beaten point of the Raz, appeared to him beneath a dazzling sun in the rosy season of heather.

"Do you think," he asked, "if I'm not punished, that they'll give me a month's leave in two years?"

Then Étienne talked about Provence, which he had left when he was quite small. The daylight was growing, and flakes of snow began to fly in the earthy sky. And at last he felt anxious on noticing Jeanlin, who was prowling about in the midst of the bushes, stupefied to see him up there. The child was beckoning to him. What was the good of this dream of fraternizing with the soldiers? It would take years and years, and his useless attempt cast him down as though he had expected to succeed. But suddenly he understood Jeanlin's gesture. The sentinel was about to be relieved, and he went away, running off to bury himself at Réquillart, his heart crushed once more by the certainty of defeat; while the little scamp who ran beside him was accusing that dirty beast of a trooper of having called out the guard to fire at them.

On the summit of the pit-bank Jules stood motionless, with eyes vacantly gazing at the falling snow. The sergeant was approaching with his men, and the regulation cries were exchanged.

"Qui vive? – Advance and give the password!"

And they heard the heavy steps begin again, ringing as though on a conquered country. In spite of the growing daylight, nothing stirred in the settlements; the colliers remained in silent rage beneath the military boot.

Chapter 2

SNOW had been falling for two days; since the morning it had ceased, and an intense frost had frozen the immense sheet. This black country, with its inky roads and walls and trees powdered with coal dust, was now white, a single whiteness stretching out without end. The Deux-Cent-Quarante settlement lay beneath the snow as though it had disappeared. No smoke came out of the chimneys; the houses, without fire and as cold as the stones in the street, did not melt the thick layer on the tiles. It was nothing more than a quarry of white slabs in the white plain, a vision of a dead village wound in its shroud. Along the roads the passing patrols alone made a muddy mess with their stamping.

Among the Maheus the last shovelful of cinders had been burnt the evening before, and it was no use any longer to think of gleaning on the pit-bank in this terrible weather, when the sparrows themselves could not find a blade of grass. Alzire, from the obstinacy with which her poor hands had dug in the snow, was dying. Maheude had to wrap her up in the fragment of a coverlet while waiting for Dr. Vanderhaghen, for whom she had twice gone out without being able to find him. The servant had, however, promised that he would come to the settlement before night, and the mother was standing at the window watching, while the little invalid, who had wished to be downstairs, was shivering on a chair, having the illusion that it was better there near the cold grate. Old Bonnemort opposite, his legs bad once more, seemed to be sleeping; neither Lénore nor Henri had come back from scouring the roads, in company with Jeanlin, to ask for sous. Maheu alone was walking heavily up and down the bare room, stumbling against the wall at every turn, with the stupid air of an animal which can no longer see its cage. The petroleum also was finished; but the reflection of the snow from outside was so bright that it vaguely lit up the room, in spite of the deepening night.

There was a noise of sabots, and the Levaque woman pushed open the door like a gale of wind, beside herself, shouting furiously from the threshold at Maheude:

"Then it's you who have said that I forced my lodger to give me twenty sous when he sleeps with me?"

The other shrugged her shoulders.

"Don't bother me. I said nothing; and who told you so?"

"They tell me you said so; it doesn't concern you who it was. You even said you could hear us at our dirty tricks behind the wall, and that the filth gets into our house because I'm always on my back. Just tell me you didn't say so, eh?"

Every day quarrels broke out as a result of the constant gossiping of the women. Especially between those households which lived door to door, squabbles and reconciliations took place every day. But never before had such bitterness thrown them one against the other. Since the strike hunger exasperated their rancour, so that they felt the need of blows; an altercation between two gossiping women finished by a murderous onset between their two men.

Just then Levaque arrived in his turn, dragging Bouteloup.

"Here's our mate; let him just say if he has given twenty sous to my wife to sleep with her."

The lodger, hiding his timid gentleness in his great beard, protested and stammered:

"Oh, that? No! Never anything! never!"

At once Levaque became threatening, and thrust his fist beneath Maheu's nose.

"You know that won't do for me. If a man's got a wife like that, he ought to knock her ribs in. If not, then you believe what she says."

"By God!" exclaimed Maheu, furious at being dragged out of his dejection, "what is all this clatter again? Haven't we got enough to do with our misery? Just leave me alone, damn you! or I'll let you know it! And first, who says that my wife said so?"

"Who says so? Pierronne said so."

Maheude broke into a sharp laugh, and turning towards the Levaque woman:

"An! Pierronne, is it? Well! I can tell you what she told me. Yes, she told me that you sleep with both your men – the one underneath and the other on top!"

After that it was no longer possible to come to an understanding. They all grew angry, and the Levaques, as a reply to the Maheus, asserted that Pierronne had said a good many other things on their account; that they had sold Catherine, that they were all rotten together, even to the little ones, with a dirty disease caught by Étienne at the Volcan.

"She said that! She said that!" yelled Maheu. "Good! I'll go to her, I will, and if she says that she said that, she shall feel my hand on her chops!"

He was carried out of himself, and the Levaques followed him to see what would happen, while Bouteloup, having a horror of disputes, furtively returned home. Excited by the altercation, Maheude was also going out, when a complaint from Alzire held her back. She crossed the ends of the coverlet over the little one's quivering body, and placed herself before the window, looking out vaguely. And that doctor, who still delayed!

At the Pierrons' door Maheu and the Levaques met Lydie, who was stamping in the snow. The house was closed, and a thread of light came though a crack in a shutter. The child replied at first to their questions with constraint: no, her father was not there, he had gone to the wash-house to join Mother Brulé and bring back the bundle of linen. Then she was confused, and would not say what her mother was doing. At last she let out everything with a sly, spiteful laugh: her mother had pushed her out of the door because M. Dansaert was there, and she prevented them from talking. Since the morning he had been going about the settlement with two policemen, trying to pick up workmen, imposing on the weak, and announcing everywhere that if the descent did not take place on Monday at the Voreux, the Company had decided to hire men from the Borinage. And as the night came on he sent away the policemen, finding Pierronne alone; then he had remained with her to drink a glass of gin before a good fire.

"Hush! hold your tongue! We must see them," said Levaque, with a lewd laugh. "We'll explain everything directly. Get off with you, youngster."

Lydie drew back a few steps while he put his eye to a crack in the shutter. He stifled a low cry and his back bent with a quiver. In her turn his wife looked through, but she said, as though taken by the colic, that it was disgusting. Maheu, who had pushed her, wishing also to see, then declared that he had had enough for his money. And they began again, in a row, each taking his glance as at a peep-show. The parlour, glittering with cleanliness, was inlivened by a large fire; there were cakes on the table with a bottle and glasses, in fact quite a feast. What they saw going on in there at last exasperated the two men, who under other circumstances would have laughed over it for six months. That she should let herself be stuffed up to the neck, with her skirts in the air, was funny. But, good God! was it not disgusting to do that in front of a great fire, and to get up one's strength with biscuits, when the mates had neither a slice of bread nor a fragment of coal?

"Here's father!" cried Lydie, running away.

Pierron was quietly coming back from the wash-house with the bundle of linen on his shoulder. Maheu immediately addressed him:

"Here! they tell me that your wife says that I sold Catherine, and that we are all rotten at home. And what do they pay you in your house, your wife and the gentleman who is this minute wearing out her skin?"

The astonished Pierron could not understand, and Pierronne, seized with fear on hearing the tumult of voices, lost her head and set the door ajar to see what was the matter. They could see her, looking very red, with her dress open and her skirt tucked up at her waist; while Dansaert, in the background, was wildly buttoning himself up. The head captain rushed away and disappeared trembling with fear that this story would reach the manager's ears. Then there would be an awful scandal, laughter, and hooting and abuse.

"You, who are always saying that other people are dirty!" shouted the Levaque woman to Pierronne; "it's not surprising that you're clean when you get the bosses to scour you."

"Ah! it's fine for her to talk!" said Levaque again. "Here's a trollop who says that my wife sleeps with me and the lodger, one below and the other above!

Yes! yes! that's what they tell me you say."

But Pierronne, grown calm, held her own against this abuse, very contemptuous in the assurance that she was the best looking and the richest.

"I've said what I've said; just leave me alone, will you! What have my affairs got to do with you, a pack of jealous creatures who want to get over us because we are able to save up money! Get along! get along! You can say what you like; my husband knows well enough why Monsieur Dansaert was here."

Pierron, in fact, was furiously defending his wife. The quarrel turned. They accused him of having sold himself, of being a spy, the Company's dog; they charged him with shutting himself up, to gorge himself with the good things with which the bosses paid him for his treachery. In defence, he pretended that Maheu had slipped beneath his door a threatening paper with two cross-bones and a dagger above. And this necessarily ended in a struggle between the men, as the quarrels of the women always did now that famine was enraging the mildest. Maheu and Levaque rushed on Pierron with their fists, and had to be pulled off.

Blood was flowing from her son-in-law's nose, when Mother Brulé, in her turn, arrived from the wash-house. When informed of what had been going on, she merely said:

"The damned beast dishonours me!"

The road was becoming deserted, not a shadow spotted the naked whiteness of the snow, and the settlement, falling back into its death-like immobility, went on starving beneath the intense cold.

"And the doctor?" asked Maheu, as he shut the door. "Not come," replied Maheude, still standing before the window.

"Are the little ones back?"

"No, not back."

Maheu again began his heavy walk from one wall to the other, looking like a stricken ox. Father Bonnemort, seated stiffly on his chair, had not even lifted his head. Alzire also had said nothing, and was trying not to shiver, so as to avoid giving them pain; but in spite of her courage in suffering, she sometimes trembled so much that one could hear against the coverlet the quivering of the little invalid girl's lean body, while with her large open eyes she stared at the ceiling, from which the pale reflection of the white gardens lit up the room like moonshine.

The emptied house was now in its last agony, having reached a final stage of nakedness. The mattress ticks had followed the wool to the dealers; then the sheets had gone, the linen, everything that could be sold. One evening they had sold a handkerchief of the grandfather's for two sous. Tears fell over each object of the poor household which had to go, and the mother was still lamenting that one day she had carried away in her skirt the pink cardboard box, her man's old present, as one would carry away a child to get rid of it on some doorstep. They were bare; they had only their skins left to sell, so worn-out and injured that no one would have given a farthing for them. They no longer even took the trouble to search, they knew that there was nothing left, that they had come to the end of everything, that they must not hope even for a candle, or a fragment of coal, or a potato, and they were waiting to die, only grieved about the children, and revolted by the useless cruelty that gave the little one a disease before starving it.

"At last! here he is!" said Maheude.

A black figure passed before the window. The door opened. But it was not Dr. Vanderhaghen; they recognized the new curé, Abbé Ranvier, who did not seem surprised at coming on this dead house, without light, without fire, without bread. He had already been to three neighbouring houses, going from family to family, seeking willing listeners, like Dansaert with his two policemen; and at once he exclaimed, in his feverish fanatic's voice:

"Why were you not at mass on Sunday, my children? You are wrong, the Church alone can save you. Now promise me to come next Sunday."

Maheu, after staring at him, went on pacing heavily, without a word. It was Maheude who replied:

"To mass, sir? What for? Isn't the good God making fun of us? Look here! what has my little girl there done to Him, to be shaking with fever? Hadn't we enough misery, that He had to make her ill too, just when I can't even give her a cup of warm gruel."

Then the priest stood and talked at length. He spoke of the strike, this terrible wretchedness, this exasperated rancour of famine, with the ardour of a missionary who is preaching to savages for the glory of religion. He said that the Church was with the poor, that she would one day cause justice to triumph by calling down the anger of God on the iniquities of the rich. And that day would come soon, for the rich had taken the place of God, and were governing without God, in their impious theft of power. But if the workers desired the fair division of the goods of the earth, they ought at once to put themselves in the hands of the priests, just as on the death of Jesus the poor and the humble grouped themselves around the apostles. What strength the pope would have, what an army the clergy would have under them, when they were able to command the numberless crowd of workers! In one week they would purge the world of the wicked, they would chase away the unworthy masters. Then, indeed, there would be a real kingdom of God, every one recompensed according to his merits, and the law of labour as the foundation for universal happiness.

Maheude, who was listening to him, seemed to hear Étienne, in those autumn evenings when he announced to them the end of their evils. Only she had always distrusted the cloth.

"That's very well, what you say there, sir," she replied, "but that's because you no longer agree with the bourgeois. All our other curés dined at the manager's, and threatened us with the devil as soon as we asked for bread."

He began again, and spoke of the deplorable misunderstanding between the Church and the people. Now, in veiled phrases, he hit at the town curés, at the bishops, at the highly placed clergy, sated with enjoyment, gorged with domination, making pacts with the liberal middle class, in the imbecility of their blindness, not seeing that it was this middle class which had dispossessed them of the empire of the world. Deliverance would come from the country priests, who would all rise to re-establish the kingdom of Christ, with the help of the poor; and already he seemed to be at their head; he raised his bony form like the chief of a band, a revolutionary of the gospel, his eyes so filled with light that they illuminated the gloomy room. This enthusiastic sermon lifted him to mystic heights, and the poor people had long ceased to understand him.

"No need for so many words," growled Maheu suddenly. "You'd best begin by bringing us a loaf."

"Come on Sunday to mass," cried the priest. "God will provide for everything."

And he went off to catechize the Levaques in their turn, so carried away by his dream of the final triumph of the Church, and so contemptuous of facts, that he would thus go through the settlements without charities, with empty hands amid this army dying of hunger, being a poor devil himself who looked upon suffering as the spur to salvation.

Maheu continued his pacing, and nothing was heard but his regular tramp which made the floor tremble. There was the sound of a rust-eaten pulley; old Bonnemort was spitting into the cold grate. Then the rhythm of the feet began again. Alzire, weakened by fever, was rambling in a low voice, laughing, thinking that it was warm and that she was playing in the sun.

"Good gracious!" muttered Maheude, after having touched her cheeks, "how she burns! I don't expect that damned beast now, the brigands must have stopped him from coming."

She meant the doctor and the Company. She uttered a joyous exclamation, however, when the door once more opened. But her arms fell back and she remained standing still with gloomy face.

"Good evening," whispered Étienne, when he had carefully closed the door.

He often came thus at night-time. The Maheus learnt his retreat after the second day. But they kept the secret and no one in the settlement knew exactly what had become of the young man. A legend had grown up around him. People still believed in him and mysterious rumours circulated: he would reappear with an army and chests full of gold; and there was always the religious expectation of a miracle, the realized ideal, a sudden entry into that city of justice which he had promised them.

Some said they had seen him lying back in a carriage, with three other gentlemen, on the Marchiennes road; others affirmed that he was in England for a few days. At length, however, suspicions began to arise and jokers accused him of hiding in a cellar, where Mouquette kept him warm; for this relationship, when known, had done him harm. There was a growing disaffection in the midst of his popularity, a gradual increase of the despairing among the faithful, and their number was certain, little by little, to grow.

"What brutal weather!" he added. "And you – nothing new, always from bad to worse? They tell me that little Négrel has been to Belgium to get Borains. Good God! we are done for if that is true!"

He shuddered as he entered this dark icy room, where it was some time before his eyes were able to see the unfortunate people whose presence he guessed by the deepening of the shade. He was experiencing the repugnance and discomfort of the workman who has risen above his class, refined by study and

stimulated by ambition. What wretchedness! and odours! and the bodies in a
heap! And a terrible pity caught him by
the throat. The spectacle of this agony so
overcame him that he tried to find words
to advise submission.

But Maheu came violently up to him,
shouting:

"Borains! They won't dare, the bloody
fools! Let the Borains go down, then, if
they want us to destroy the pits!"

With an air of constraint, Étienne
explained that it was not possible to
move, that the soldiers who guarded the
pits would protect the descent of the
Belgian workmen. And Maheu clenched
his fists, irritated especially, as he said,
by having bayonets in his back. Then the
colliers were no longer masters in their
own place? They were treated, then, like
convicts, forced to work by a loaded
musket! He loved his pit, it was a great
grief to him not to have been down for
two months. He was driven wild,
therefore, at the idea of this insult, these

strangers whom they threatened to introduce. Then the recollection that his certificate had been given back to him struck him to the heart.

"I don't know why I'm angry," he muttered. "I don't belong to their shop any longer. When they have hunted me away from here, I may as well die on the road."

"As to that," said Étienne, "if you like, they'll take your certificate back to-morrow. People don't send away good workmen."

He interrupted himself, surprised to hear Alzire, who was laughing softly in the delirium of her fever. So far he had only made out Father Bonnemort's stiff shadow, and this gaiety of the sick child frightened him. It was indeed too much if the little ones were going to die of it. With trembling voice he made up his mind.

"Look here! this can't go on, we are done for. We must give it up."

Maheude, who had been motionless and silent up to now, suddenly broke out, and treating him familiarly and swearing like a man, she shouted in his face:

"What's that you say? It's you who say that, by God!" He was about to give reasons, but she would not let him speak.

"Don't repeat that, by God! or, woman as I am, I'll put my fist into your face. Then we have been dying for two months, and I have sold my household, and my little ones have fallen ill of it, and there is to be nothing done, and the injustice is to begin again! Ah! do you know! when I think of that my blood stands still. No, no, I would burn everything, I would kill everything, rather than give up."

She pointed at Maheu in the darkness, with a vague, threatening gesture.

"Listen to this! If any man goes back to the pit, he'll find me waiting for him on the road to spit in his face and cry coward!

Étienne could not see her, but he felt a heat like the breath of a barking animal. He had drawn back, astonished at this fury which was his work. She was so changed that he could no longer recognize the woman who was once so sensible, reproving his violent schemes, saying that we ought not to wish any one dead, and who was now refusing to listen to reason and talking of killing people. It was not he now, it was she, who talked politics, who dreamed of sweeping away the bourgeois at a stroke, who demanded the republic and the guillotine to free the earth of these rich robbers who fattened on the labour of starvelings.

"Yes, I could flay them with my fingers. We've had enough of them! Our turn is come now; you used to say so yourself. When I think of the father, the grandfather, the grandfather's father, what all of them who went before have suffered, what we are suffering, and that our sons and our sons' sons will suffer it over again, it makes me mad — I could take a knife. The other day we didn't do enough at Montsou; we ought to have pulled the bloody place to the ground, down to the last brick. And do you know I've only one regret, that we didn't let the old man strangle the Piolaine girl. Hunger may strangle my little ones for all they care!"

Her words fell like the blows of an axe in the night. The closed horizon would not open, and the impossible ideal was turning to poison in the depths of this skull which had been crushed by grief.

"You have misunderstood," Étienne was able to say at last, beating a retreat. "We ought to come to an understanding with the Company. I know that the pits are suffering much, so that it would probably consent to an arrangement."

"No, never!" she shouted.

Just then Lénore and Henri came back with their hands empty. A gentleman had certainly given them two sous, but the girl kept kicking her little brother, and the two sous fell into the snow, and as

Jeanlin had joined in the search they had not been able to find them.

"Where is Jeanlin?"

"He's gone away, mother; he said he had business."

Étienne was listening with an aching heart. Once she had threatened to kill them if they ever held out their hands to beg. Now she sent them herself on to the roads, and proposed that all of them – the ten thousand colliers of Montsou – should take stick and wallet, like beggars of old, and scour the terrified country.

The anguish continued to increase in the black room. The little urchins came back hungry, they wanted to eat; why could they not have something to eat? And they grumbled, flung themselves about, and at last trod on the feet of their dying sister, who groaned. The mother furiously boxed their ears in the darkness at random. Then, as they cried still louder, asking for bread, she burst into tears, and dropped on to the floor, seizing them in one embrace with the little invalid; then, for a long time, her tears fell in a nervous outbreak which left her limp and worn out, stammering over and over again the same phrase, calling for death:

"O God! why do You not take us? O God! in pity take us, to have done with it!"

The grandfather preserved his immobility, like an old tree twisted by the rain and wind; while the father continued walking between the fireplace and the cupboard, without turning his head.

But the door opened, and this time it was Doctor Vanderhaghen.

"The devil!" he said. "This light won't spoil your eyes. Look sharp! I'm in a hurry."

As usual, he scolded, knocked up by work. Fortunately, he had matches with him, and the father had to strike six, one by one, and to hold them while he examined the invalid. Unwound from her coverlet, she shivered beneath this flickering light, as lean as a bird dying in the snow, so small that one only saw her hump. But she smiled with the wandering smile of the dying, and her eyes were very large; while her poor hands contracted over her hollow breast. And as the half-choked mother asked if it was right to take away from her the only child who helped in the household, so intelligent and gentle, the doctor grew vexed.

"Ah! she is going. Dead of hunger, your blessed child. And not the only one, either; I've just seen another one over there. You all send for me, but I can't do anything; it's meat that you want to cure you."

Maheu, with burnt fingers, had dropped the match, and the darkness closed over the little corpse, which was still warm. The doctor had gone away in a hurry. Étienne heard nothing more in the black room but Maheude's sobs, repeating her cry for death, that melancholy and endless lamentation:

"O God! it is my turn, take me! O God! take my man, take the others, out of pity, to have done with it!"

The grandfather preserved his immobility, like an old tree twisted by the rain and wind; while the father continued walking between the fireplace and the cupboard, without turning his head.

But the door opened, and this time it was Doctor Vanderhaghen.

"The devil!" he said. "This light won't spoil your eyes. Look sharp! I'm in a hurry."

As usual, he scolded, knocked up by work. Fortunately, he had matches with him, and the father had to strike six, one by one, and to hold them while he examined the invalid. Unwound from her coverlet, she shivered beneath this flickering light, as lean as a bird dying in the snow, so small that one only saw her hump. But she smiled with the wandering smile of the dying, and her eyes were very large; while her poor hands contracted over her hollow breast. And as the half-choked mother asked if it was right to take away from her the only child who helped in the household, so intelligent and gentle, the doctor grew vexed.

"Ah! she is going. Dead of hunger, your blessed child. And not the only one, either; I've just seen another one over there. You all send for me, but I can't do anything; it's meat that you want to cure you."

Maheu, with burnt fingers, had dropped the match, and the darkness closed over the little corpse, which was still warm. The doctor had gone away in a hurry. Étienne heard nothing more in the black room but Maheude's sobs, repeating her cry for death, that melancholy and endless lamentation:

"O God! it is my turn, take me! O God! take my man, take the others, out of pity, to have done with it!"

Chapter 3

ON that Sunday, ever since eight o'clock, Souvarine had been sitting alone in the parlour of the Avantage, at his accustomed place, with his head against the wall. Not a single collier knew where to get two sous for a drink, and never had the bars had fewer customers. So Madame Rasseneur, motionless at the counter, preserved an irritated silence; while Rasseneur, standing before the iron fireplace, seemed to be gazing with a reflective air at the brown smoke from the coal.

Suddenly, in this heavy silence of an over-heated room, three light quick blows struck against one of the windowpanes made Souvarine turn his head. He rose, for he recognized the signal which Étienne had already used several times before, in order to call him, when he saw him from without, smoking his cigarette at an empty table. But before the engine-man could reach the door, Rasseneur had opened it, and, recognizing the man who stood there in the light from the window, he said to him:

"Are you afraid that I shall sell you? You can talk better here than on the road."

Étienne entered. Madame Rasseneur politely offered him a glass, which he refused, with a gesture. The innkeeper added:

"I guessed long ago where you hide yourself. If I was a spy, as your friends say, I should have sent the police after you a week ago."

"There is no need for you to defend yourself," replied the young man. "I know that you have never eaten that sort of bread. People may have different ideas and esteem each other all the same."

And there was silence once more. Souvarine had gone back to his chair, with his back to the wall and his eyes fixed on the smoke from his cigarette, but his feverish fingers were moving restlessly, and he ran them over his knees, seeking the warm fur of Poland, who was absent this evening; it was an unconscious discomfort, something that was lacking, he could not exactly say what.

Seated on the other side of the table, Étienne at last said:

"To-morrow work begins again at the Voreux. The Belgians have come with little Négrel."

"Yes, they landed them at nightfall," muttered Rasseneur, who remained standing. "As long as they don't kill each other after all!"

Then raising his voice:

"No, you know, I don't want to begin our disputes over again, but this will end badly if you hold out any longer. Why, your story is just like that of your International. I met Pluchart the day before yesterday, at Lille, where I went on business. It's going wrong, that machine of his."

He gave details. The association, after having conquered the workers of the whole world, in an outburst of propaganda which had left the middle class still shuddering, was now being devoured and slowly destroyed by an internal struggle between vanities and ambitions. Since the anarchists had triumphed in it, chasing out the earlier evolutionists, everything was breaking up; the original aim, the reform of the wage-system, was lost in the midst of the squabbling of sects; the scientific framework was disorganized by the hatred of discipline. And already it was possible to foresee the final miscarriage of this general revolt which for a moment had threatened to carry away in a breath the old rotten society.

"Pluchart is ill over it," Rasseneur went on. "And he has no voice at all now. All the same, he talks on in spite of everything and wants to go to Paris. And he told me three times over that our strike was done for."

Étienne with his eyes on the ground let him talk on without interruption. The evening before he had chatted with some mates, and he felt that breaths of spite and suspicion were passing over him, those first breaths of unpopularity which forerun defeat. And he remained gloomy, he would not confess dejection in the presence of a man who had foretold to him that the crowd would hoot him in his turn on the day when they had to avenge themselves for a miscalculation.

"No doubt the strike is done for, I know that as well as Pluchart," he said. "But we foresaw that. We accepted this strike against our wishes, we didn't count on finishing up with the Company. Only one gets carried away, one begins to expect things, and when it turns out badly one forgets that one ought to have expected that, instead of lamenting and quarrelling as if it were a catastrophe tumbled down from heaven."

"Then if you think the game's lost," asked Rasseneur, "why don't you make the mates listen to reason?"

The young man looked at him fixedly.

"Listen! enough of this. You have your ideas, I have mine. I came in here to show you that I feel esteem for you in spite of everything. But I still think that if we come to grief over this trouble, our starved carcasses will do more for the people's cause than all your common-sense politics. Ah! if one of those bloody soldiers would just put a bullet in my heart, that would be a fine way of ending!"

His eyes were moist, as in this cry there broke out the secret desire of the vanquished, the refuge in which he desired to lose his torment for ever.

"Well said!" declared Madame Rasseneur, casting on her husband a look which was full of all the contempt of her radical opinions.

Souvarine, with a vague gaze, feeling about with his nervous hands, did not appear to hear. His fair girlish face, with the thin nose and small pointed teeth, seemed to be growing savage in some mystic dream full of bloody visions. And he began to dream aloud, replying to a remark of Rasseneur's about the International which had been let fall in the course of the conversation.

"They are all cowards; there is only one man who can make their machine into a terrible instrument of destruction. It requires will, and none of them have will; and that's why the revolution will miscarry once more."

He went on in a voice of disgust, lamenting the imbecility of men, while the other two were disturbed by these somnambulistic confidences made in the darkness. In Russia there was nothing going on well, and he was in despair over the news he had received. His old companions were all turning to the politicians; the famous Nihilists who made Europe tremble – sons of village priests, of the lower middle class, of tradesmen – could not rise above the idea of national liberation, and seemed to believe that the world would be delivered – when they had killed their despot. As soon as he spoke to them of razing society to the ground like a ripe harvest – as soon as he even pronounced the infantile word "republic" – he felt that he was misunderstood and a disturber, henceforth unclassed, enrolled among the lost leaders of cosmopolitan revolution. His patriotic heart struggled, however, and it was with painful bitterness that he repeated his favourite expression:

"Foolery! They'll never get out of it with their foolery."

Then, lowering his voice still more, in a few bitter words he described his old dream of fraternity. He had renounced his rank and his fortune; he had gone among workmen, only in the hope of seeing at last the foundation of a new society of labour in common. All the sous in his pockets had long gone to the urchins of the settlement; he had been as tender as a brother with the colliers, smiling at their suspicion, winning them over by his quiet workmanlike ways and his dislike of chattering. But decidedly the fusion had not taken place; he remained a stranger, with his contempt of all bonds, his desire to keep himself free of all petty vanities and enjoyments. And since this morning he had been especially exasperated by reading an incident in the newspapers.

His voice changed, his eyes grew bright, he fixed them on Étienne, directly addressing him:

"Now, do you understand that? These hatworkers at Marseilles who have won the great lottery prize of a hundred thousand francs have gone off at once and invested it, declaring that they are going to live without doing anything! Yes, that is your idea, all of you French workmen; you want to unearth a treasure in order to devour it alone afterwards in some lazy, selfish corner. You may cry out as much as you like against the rich, you haven't got courage enough to give back to the poor the money that luck brings you. You will never be worthy of happiness as long as you own anything, and your hatred of the bourgeois proceeds solely from an angry desire to be bourgeois yourselves in their place."

Rasseneur burst out laughing. The idea that the two Marseilles workmen ought to renounce the big prize seemed to him absurd. But Souvarine grew pale; his face changed and became terrible in one of those religious rages which exterminate nations. He cried:

"You will all be mown down, overthrown, cast on the dung-heap. Someone will be born who will annihilate your race of cowards and pleasure-seekers. And look here! you see my hands; if my hands were able they would take up the earth, like that, and shake it until it was smashed to fragments, and you were all buried beneath the rubbish."

"Well said," declared Madame Rasseneur, with her polite and convinced air.

There was silence again. Then Étienne spoke once more of the Borinage men. He questioned Souvarine concerning the steps that had been taken at the Voreux. But the engine-man was still preoccupied, and scarcely replied. He only knew that cartridges would be distributed to the soldiers who were guarding the pit; and the nervous restlessness of his fingers over his knees increased to such an extent that, at last, he became conscious of what was lacking – the soft and soothing fur of the tame rabbit.

"Where is Poland, then?" he asked.

The innkeeper laughed again as he looked at his wife. After an awkward silence he made up his mind:

"Poland? She is in the pot."

Since her adventure with Jeanlin, the pregnant rabbit, no doubt wounded, had only brought forth dead young ones; and to avoid feeding a useless mouth they had resigned themselves that very day to serve her up with potatoes.

"Yes, you ate one of her legs this evening. Eh! You licked your fingers after it!"

Souvarine had not understood at first. Then he became very pale, and his face contracted with nausea; while, in spite of his stoicism, two large tears were swelling beneath his eyelids.

But no one had time to notice this emotion, for the door had opened roughly and Chaval had appeared, pushing Catherine before him. After having made himself drunk with beer and bluster in all the public-houses of Montsou, the idea had occurred to him to go to the Avantage to show his old friends that he was not afraid. As he came in, he said to his mistress:

"By God! I tell you you shall drink a glass in here; I'll break the jaws of the first man who looks askance at me!"

Catherine, moved at the sight of Étienne, had become very pale. When Chaval in his turn perceived him, he grinned in his evil fashion.

"Two glasses, Madame Rasseneur! We're wetting the new start of work."

Without a word she poured out, as a woman who never refused her beer to any one. There was silence, and neither the landlord nor the two others stirred from their places.

"I know people who've said that I was a spy," Chaval went on swaggeringly, "and I'm waiting for them just to say it again to my face, so that we can have a bit of explanation."

No one replied, and the men turned their heads and gazed vaguely at the walls.

"There are some who sham, and there are some who don't sham," he went on louder. "I've nothing to hide. I've left Deneulin's dirty shop, and to-morrow I'm going down to the Voreux with a dozen Belgians, who have been given me to lead because I'm held in esteem; and if any one doesn't like that, he can just say so, and we'll talk it over."

Then, as the same contemptuous silence greeted his provocations, he turned furiously on Catherine.

"Will you drink, by God? Drink with me to the confusion of all the dirty beasts who refuse to work."

She drank, but with so trembling a hand that the two glasses struck together with a tinkling sound. He had now pulled out of his pocket a handful of silver, which he exhibited with drunken ostentation, saying that he had earned that with his sweat, and that he defied the shammers to show ten sous. The attitude of his mates exasperated him, and he began to come to direct insults.

"Then it is at night that the moles come out? The police have to go to sleep before we meet the brigands."

Étienne had risen, very calm and resolute.

"Listen! You annoy me. Yes, you are a spy; your money still stinks of some treachery. You've sold yourself, and it disgusts me to touch your skin. No matter; I'm your man. It is quite time that one of us did for the other."

Chaval clenched his fists.

"Come along, then, cowardly dog! I must call you so to warm you up. You all alone – I'm quite willing; and you shall pay for all the bloody tricks that have been played on me."

With suppliant arms Catherine advanced between them. But they had no need to repel her; she felt the necessity of the battle, and slowly drew back of her own accord. Standing against the wall, she remained silent, so paralysed with anguish that she no longer shivered, her large eyes gazing at these two men who were going to kill each other over her.

Madame Rasseneur simply removed the glasses from the counter for fear that they might be broken. Then she sat down again on the bench, without showing any improper curiosity. But two old mates could not be left to murder each other like this. Rasseneur persisted in interfering, and Souvarine had to take him by the shoulder and lead him back to the table, saying:

"It doesn't concern you. There is one of them too many, and the strongest must live."

Without waiting for the attack, Chaval's fists were already dealing blows at space. He was the taller of the two, and his blows swung about aiming at the face, with furious cutting movements of both arms one after the other, as though he were handling a couple of sabres. And he went on talking, playing to the gallery with volleys of abuse, which served to excite him.

"Ah! you damned devil, I'll have your nose! I'll do for your bloody nose! Just let me get at your chops, you whores' looking-glass; I'll make a hash of it for the pigs and then we shall see if the strumpets will run after you!"

In silence, and with clenched teeth, Étienne gathered up his small figure, according to the rules of the game, protecting his chest and face by both fists; and he watched and let them fly like springs released, with terrible straight blows.

At first they did each other little damage. The whirling and blustering blows of the one, the cool watchfulness of the other, prolonged the struggle. A chair was overthrown; their heavy boots crushed the white sand scattered on the floor. But at last they were out of breath, their panting respiration was heard, while their faces became red and swollen as from an interior fire which flamed out from the clear holes of their eyes.

"Played!" yelled Chaval; "trumps on your carcass!"

In fact his fist, working like a flail, had struck his adversary's shoulder. Étienne restrained a groan of pain and the only sound that was heard was the dull bruising of the muscles. Étienne replied with a straight blow to Chaval's chest, which would have knocked him out, had he had not saved himself by one of his constant goat-like leaps. The blow, however, caught him on the left flank with such effect that he tottered, momentarily winded. He became furious on feeling his arm grow limp with pain, and kicked out like a wild beast, aiming at his adversary's belly with his heel.

"Have at your guts!" he stammered in a choked voice. "I'll pull them out and unwind them for you!"

Étienne avoided the blow, so indignant at this infraction of the laws of fair fighting that he broke silence.

"Hold your tongue, brute! And no feet, by God! or I take a chair and bash you with it!"

Then the struggle became serious. Rasseneur was disgusted, and would again have interfered, but a severe look from his wife held him back: had not two customers a right to settle an affair in the house? He simply placed himself before the fireplace, for fear lest they should tumble over into it. Souvarine, in his quiet way, had rolled a cigarette, but he forgot to light it. Catherine was motionless against the wall; only her hands had unconsciously risen to her waist, and with constant fidgeting movements were twisting and tearing at the stuff of her dress. She was striving as hard as possible not to cry out, and so, perhaps, kill one of them by declaring her preference; but she was, too, so distracted that she did not even know which she preferred.

Chaval, who was bathed in sweat and striking at random, soon became exhausted. In spite of his anger, Étienne continued to cover himself, parrying nearly all the blows, a few of which grazed him. His ear was split, a finger nail had torn away a piece of his neck, and this so smarted that he swore in his turn as he drove out one of his terrible straight blows. Once more Chaval saved his chest by a leap, but he had lowered himself, and the fist reached his face, smashing his nose and crushing one eye. Immediately a jet of blood came from his nostrils, and his eye became swollen and bluish. Blinded by this red flood, and dazed by the shock to his skull, the wretch was beating the air with his arms at random, when another blow, striking him at last full in the chest, finished him. There was a crunching sound; he fell on his back with a heavy thud, as when a sack of plaster is emptied.

Étienne waited.

"Get up! if you want some more, we'll begin again." Without replying, Chaval, after a few minutes' stupefaction, moved on the ground and stretched his limbs. He picked himself up with difficulty, resting for a moment curled up on his knees, doing something with his hand in the bottom of his pocket which could not be observed. Then, when he was up, he rushed forward again, his throat swelling with a savage yell.

But Catherine had seen; and in spite of herself a loud cry came from her heart, astonishing her like the avowal of a preference she had herself been ignorant of:

"Take care! he's got his knife!"

Étienne had only time to parry the first blow with his arm. His woollen jacket was cut by the thick blade, one of those blades fastened by a copper ferrule into a boxwood handle. He had already seized Chaval's wrist, and a terrible struggle began; for he felt that he would be lost if he let go, while the other shook his arm in the effort to free it and strike. The weapon was gradually lowered as their stiffened limbs grew fatigued. Étienne twice felt the cold sensation of the steel against his skin; and he had to make a supreme effort, so crushing the other's wrist that the knife slipped from his hand. Both of them had fallen to the earth, and it was Étienne who snatched it up, brandishing it in his turn. He held Chaval down beneath his knee and threatened to slit his throat open.

"Ah, traitor! by God! you've got it coming to you now!"

He felt an awful voice within, deafening him. It arose from his bowels and was beating in his head like a hammer, a sudden mania of murder, a need to taste blood. Never before had the crisis so shaken him. He was not drunk, however, and he struggled against the hereditary disease with the despairing shudder of a man who is mad with lust and struggles on the verge of rape. At last he conquered himself; he threw the knife behind him, stammering in a hoarse voice:

"Get up – off you go!"

This time Rasseneur had rushed forward, but without quite daring to venture between them, for fear of catching a nasty blow. He did not want any one to be murdered in his house, and was so angry that his wife, sitting erect at the counter, remarked to him that he always cried out too soon. Souvarine. who had nearly caught the knife in his legs, decided to light his cigarette. Was it, then, all over?

Catherine was looking on stupidly at the two men, who were unexpectedly both living.

"Off you go!" repeated Étienne. "Off you go, or I'll do for you!"

Chaval arose, and with the back of his hand wiped away the blood which continued to flow from his nose; with jaw smeared red and bruised eye, he went away trailing his feet, furious at his defeat. Catherine mechanically followed him. Then he turned round, and his hatred broke out in a flood of filth.

"No, no! since you want him, sleep with him, dirty jade! and don't put your bloody feet in my place again if you value your skin!"

He violently banged the door. There was deep silence in the warm room, the low crackling of the coal was alone heard. On the ground there only remained the overturned chair and a rain of blood which the sand on the floor was drinking up.

Chapter 4

WHEN they came out of Rasseneur's, Étienne and Catherine walked on in silence. The thaw was beginning, a slow cold thaw which stained the snow without melting it. In the livid sky a full moon could be faintly seen behind great clouds, black rags driven furiously by a tempestuous wind far above; and on the earth no breath was stirring, nothing could be heard but drippings from the roofs, the falling of white lumps with a soft thud.

Étienne was embarrassed by this woman who had been given to him, and in his disquiet he could find nothing to say. The idea of taking her with him to hide at Réquillart seemed absurd. He had proposed to lead her back to the settlement, to her parents' house, but she had refused in terror. No, no! anything rather than be a burden on them once more after having behaved so badly to them! And neither of them spoke any more; they tramped on at random through the roads which were becoming rivers of mud. At first they went down towards the Voreux; then they turned to the right and passed between the pit-bank and the canal.

"But you'll have to sleep somewhere," he said at last. "Now, if I only had a room, I could easily take you–"

But a curious spasm of timidity interrupted him. The past came back to him, their old longings for each other, and the delicacies and the shames which had prevented them from coming together. Did he still desire her, that he felt so troubled, gradually warmed at the heart by a fresh longing? The recollection of the blows she had dealt him at Gaston-Marie now attracted him instead of filling him with spite. And he was surprised; the idea of taking her to Réquillart was becoming quite natural and easy to execute.

"Now, come, decide; where would you like me to take you? You must hate me very much to refuse to come with me!"

She was following him slowly, delayed by the painful slipping of her sabots into the ruts; and without raising her head she murmured:

"I have enough trouble, good God! don't give me any more. What good would it do us, what you ask, now that I have a lover and you have a woman yourself?"

She meant Mouquette. She believed that he still went with this girl, as the rumour ran for the last fortnight; and when he swore to her that it was not so she shook her head, for she remembered the evening when she had seen them eagerly kissing each other.

"Isn't it a pity, all this nonsense?" he whispered, stopping. "We might under-stand each other so well."

She shuddered slightly and replied:

"Never mind, you've nothing to be sorry for; you don't lose much. If you knew what a trumpery thing I am – no bigger than two ha'porth of butter, so ill made that I shall never become a woman, sure enough!"

And she went on freely accusing herself, as though the long delay of her puberty had been her own fault. In spite of the man whom she had had, this lessened her, placed her among the urchins. One has some excuse, at any rate, when one can produce a child.

"My poor little one!" said Étienne, with deep pity, in a very low voice.

They were at the foot of the pit-bank, hidden in the shadow of the enormous pile. An inky cloud was just then passing over the moon; they could no longer even distinguish their faces, their breaths were mingled, their lips were seeking each other for that kiss which had tormented them with desire for months. But suddenly the moon reappeared, and they saw the sentinel above them, at the top of the rocks white with light, standing out erect on the Voreux. And before they had kissed an emotion of modesty separated them, that old modesty in which there was something of anger, a vague repugnance, and much friendship. They set out again heavily, up to their ankles in mud.

"Then it's settled. You don't want to have anything to do with me?" asked Étienne.

"No," she said. "You after Chaval; and after you another, eh? No, that disgusts me; it doesn't give me any pleasure. What's the use of doing it?"

They were silent, and walked some hundred paces without exchanging a word.

"But, anyhow, do you know where to go to?" he said again. "I can't leave you out in a night like this."

She replied, simply:

"I'm going back. Chaval is my man. I have nowhere else to sleep but with him."

"But he will beat you to death."

There was silence again. She had shrugged her shoulders in resignation. He would beat her, and when he was tired of beating her he would stop. Was not that better than to roam the streets like a vagabond? Then she was used to blows; she said, to console herself, that eight out of ten girls were no better off than she was. If her lover married her some day it would, all the same, be very nice of him.

Étienne and Catherine were moving mechanically towards Montsou, and as they came nearer their silences grew longer. It was as though they had never before been together. He could find no argument to convince her, in spite of the deep vexation which he felt at seeing her go back to Chaval. His heart was breaking, he had nothing better to offer than an existence of wretchedness and flight, a night with no tomorrow should a soldier's bullet go through his head. Perhaps, after all, it was wiser to suffer what he was suffering rather than risk a fresh suffering. So he led her back to her lover's, with sunken head, and made no protest when she stopped him on the main road, at the corner of the Yards, twenty metres from the Estaminet Piquette, saying:

"Don't come any farther. If he sees you it will only make things worse."

Eleven o'clock struck at the church. The estaminet was closed, but gleams came through the cracks.

"Good-bye," she murmured.

She had given him her hand; he kept it, and she had to draw it away painfully, with a slow effort, to leave him. Without turning her head, she went in through the little latched door. But he did not turn away, standing at the same place with his eyes on the house, anxious as to what was passing within. He listened, trembling lest he should hear the cries of a beaten woman. The house remained black and silent; he only saw a light appear at a first-floor window, and as this window opened, and he recognized the thin shadow that was leaning over the road, he came near.

Catherine then whispered very low:

"He's not come back. I'm going to bed. Please go away."

Étienne went off. The thaw was increasing; a regular shower was falling from the roofs, a moist sweat flowed down the walls, the palings, the whole confused mass of this industrial district lost in night. At first he turned towards Réquillart, sick with fatigue and sadness, having no other desire except to disappear under the earth and to be annihilated there. Then the idea of the Voreux occurred to him again. He thought of the Belgian workmen who were going down, of his mates at the settlement, exasperated against the soldiers and resolved not to tolerate strangers in their pit. And he passed again along the canal through the puddles of melted snow.

As he stood once more near the pit-bank the moon was shining brightly. He raised his eyes and gazed at the sky. The clouds were galloping by, whipped on by the strong wind which was blowing up there; but they were growing white, and ravelling out thinly with the misty transparency of troubled water over the moon's face. They succeeded each other so rapidly that the moon, veiled at moments, constantly reappeared in limpid clearness.

With gaze full of this pure brightness, Étienne was lowering his head, when a spectacle on the summit of the pit-bank attracted his attention. The sentinel, stiffened by cold, was walking up and down, taking twenty-five paces towards Marchiennes, and then returning towards Montsou. The white glitter of his bayonet could be seen above his black silhouette, which stood out clearly against the pale sky. But what interested the young man, behind the cabin where Bonnemort used to take shelter on tempestuous nights, was a moving shadow – a crouching beast in ambush – which he immediately recognized as Jeanlin, with his long flexible spine like a marten's. The sentinel could not see him. That brigand of a child was certainly preparing some practical joke, for he was still furious against the soldiers, and asking when they were going to be freed from these murderers who had been sent here with guns to kill people.

For a moment Étienne thought of calling him to prevent the execution of some stupid trick. The moon was hidden. He had seen him draw himself up ready to spring; but the moon reappeared, and the child remained crouching. At every turn the sentinel came as far as the cabin, then turned his back and walked in the opposite direction. And suddenly, as a cloud threw its shadow, Jeanlin leapt on to the soldier's shoulders with the great bound of a wild cat, and gripping him with his claws buried his large open knife in his throat. The horse-hair collar resisted; he had to apply both hands to the handle and hang on with all the weight of his body. He had often bled fowls which he had found behind farms. It was so rapid that there was only a stifled cry in the night, while the musket fell with the sound of old iron. Already the moon was shining again.

Motionless with stupor, Étienne was still gazing. A shout had been choked in his chest. Above, the pit-bank was vacant; no shadow was any longer visible against the wild flight of clouds. He ran up and found Jeanlin on all fours before the corpse, which was lying back with extended arms. Beneath the limpid light the red trousers and grey overcoat contrasted harshly with the snow. Not a drop of blood had flowed, the knife was still in the throat up to the handle. With a furious, unreasoning blow of the fist he knocked the child down beside the body.

"What have you done that for?" he stammered wildly. Jeanlin picked himself up and rested on his hands, with a feline movement of his thin spine; his large ears, his green eyes, his prominent jaws were quivering and aflame with the shock of his deadly blow.

"By God! why have you done this?"

"I don't know; I wanted to."

He persisted in this reply. For three days he had wanted to. It tormented him, it made his head ache behind his ears, because he thought about it so much. Need one be so particular with these damned soldiers who were worrying the colliers in their own homes? Of the violent speeches he had heard in the forest, the cries of destruction and death shouted among the pits, five or six words had remained with him, and these he repeated like a street urchin playing at revolution. And he knew no more; no one had urged him on, it had come to him of itself, just as the desire to steal onions from a field came to him.

Startled at this obscure growth of crime in the recesses of this childish brain, Étienne again pushed him away with a kick, like an unconscious animal. He trembled lest the guard at the Voreux had heard the sentinel's stifled cry, and looked towards the pit every time the moon was uncovered. But nothing stirred, and he bent down, felt the hands that were gradually becoming icy, and listened to the heart, which had stopped beneath the overcoat. Only the bone handle of the knife could be seen with the motto on it, the simple word "Amour," engraved in black letters.

His eyes went from the throat to the face. Suddenly he recognized the little soldier; it was Jules, the recruit with whom he had talked one morning. And deep pity came over him in front of this fair gentle face, marked with freckles. The blue eyes, wide open, were gazing at the sky with that fixed gaze with which he had before seen him searching the horizon for the country of his birth. Where was it, that Plogof which had appeared to him beneath the dazzling sun? Over there, over there! The sea was moaning afar on this tempestuous night. That wind passing above had perhaps swept over the moors. Two women perhaps were standing there, the mother and the sister, clutching their wind-blown coifs, gazing as if they could see what was now happening to the little fellow through the leagues which separated them. They would always wait for him now. What an abominable thing it is for poor devils to kill each other for the sake of the rich!

But this corpse had to be disposed of. Étienne at first thought of throwing it into the canal, but was deterred from this by the certainty that it would be found there. His anxiety became extreme, every minute was of importance; what decision should he take? He had a sudden inspiration: if he could carry the body as far as Réquillart, he would be able to bury it there for ever.

"Come here," he said to Jeanlin.

The child was suspicious.

"No, you want to beat me. And then I have business. Good night."

In fact, he had given a rendezvous to Bébert and Lydie in a hiding-place, a hole arranged under the wood supply at the Voreux. It had been arranged to sleep out, so as to be there if the Belgians' bones were to be broken by stoning when they went down the pit.

"Listen!" repeated Étienne. "Come here, or I shall call the soldiers, who will cut your head off."

And as Jeanlin was making up his mind, he rolled his handkerchief, and bound the soldier's neck tightly, without drawing out the knife, so as to prevent the blood from flowing. The snow was melting; on the soil there was neither a red patch nor the footmarks of a struggle.

"Take the legs!"

Jeanlin took the legs, while Étienne seized the shoulders, after having fastened the gun behind his back, and then they both slowly descended the pit-bank, trying to avoid rolling any rocks down. Fortunately the moon was hidden. But as they passed along the canal it reappeared brightly, and it was a miracle that the guard did not see them. Silently they hastened on, hindered by the swinging of the corpse, and obliged to place it on the ground every hundred metres. At the corner of the Réquillart lane they heard a sound which froze them with terror, and they only had time to hide behind a wall to avoid a patrol. Farther on, a man came across them, but he was drunk, and moved away abusing them. At last they reached the old pit, bathed in perspiration, and so exhausted that their teeth were chattering.

Étienne had guessed that it would not be easy to get the soldier down the ladder shaft. It was an awful task. First of all Jeanlin, standing above, had to let the body slide down, while Étienne, hanging on to the bushes, had to accompany it to enable it to pass the first two ladders where the rungs were broken. Afterwards, at every ladder, he had to perform the same manoeuvre over again, going down first, then receiving the body in his arms; and he had thus, down thirty ladders, two hundred and ten metres, to feel it constantly falling over him. The gun scraped his spine; he had not allowed the child to go for the candle-end, which he preserved avariciously. What was the use? The light would only embarrass them in this narrow tube. When they arrived at the pit-eye, however, out of breath, he sent the youngster for the candle. He then sat down and waited for him in the darkness, near the body, with heart beating violently. As soon as Jeanlin reappeared with the light, Étienne consulted with him, for the child had explored these old workings, even to the cracks through which men could not pass. They set out again, dragging the dead body for nearly a kilometre, through a maze of ruinous galleries. At last the roof became low, and they found themselves kneeling beneath a sandy rock supported by half-broken planks. It was a sort of long chest in which they laid the little soldier as in a coffin; they placed his gun by his side; then with vigorous blows of their heels they broke the timber at the risk of being buried themselves. Immediately the rock gave way, and they scarcely had time to crawl back on their elbows and knees. When Étienne returned, seized by the desire to look once more, the roof was still falling in, slowly crushing the body beneath its enormous weight. And then there was nothing more left, nothing but the vast mass of the earth.

Jeanlin, having returned to his own corner, his little cavern of villainy, was stretching himself out on the hay, overcome by weariness, and murmuring:

"Heighho! the brats must wait for me; I'm going to have an hour's sleep."

Étienne had blown out the candle, of which there was only a small end left. He also was worn out, but he was not sleepy; painful nightmare thoughts were beating like hammers in his skull. Only one at last remained, torturing him and fatiguing him with a question to which he could not reply: Why had he not struck Chaval when he held him beneath the knife? and why had this child just killed a soldier whose very name he did not know? It shook his revolutionary beliefs, the courage to kill, the right to kill. Was he, then, a coward? In the hay the child had begun snoring, the snoring of a drunken man, as if he were sleeping off the intoxication of his murder. Étienne was disgusted and irritated; it hurt him to know that the boy was there and to hear him. Suddenly he started, a breath of fear passed over his face. A light rustling, a sob, seemed to him to have come out of the depths of the earth. The image of the little soldier, lying over there with his gun beneath the rocks, froze his back and made his hair stand up. It was idiotic, the whole mine seemed to be filled with voices; he had to light the candle again, and only grew calm on seeing the emptiness of the galleries by this pale light.

For another quarter of an hour he reflected, still absorbed in the same struggle, his eyes fixed on the burning wick. But there was a spluttering, the wick was going out, and everything fell back into darkness. He shuddered again; he could have boxed Jeanlin's ears, to keep him from snoring so loudly. The neighbourhood of the child became so unbearable that he escaped, tormented by the need for fresh air, hastening through the galleries and up the passage, as though he could hear a shadow, panting, at his heels.

Up above, in the midst of the ruins of Réquillart, Étienne was at last able to breathe freely. Since he dared not kill, it was for him to die; and this idea of death, which had already touched him, came again and fixed itself in his head, as a last hope. To die bravely, to die for the revolution, that would end everything, would settle his account, good or bad, and prevent him from thinking more. If the men attacked the Borains, he would be in the first rank, and would have a good chance of getting a bad blow. It was with firmer step that he returned to prowl around the Voreux. Two o'clock struck, and the loud noise of voices was coming from the captains' room, where the guards who watched over the pit were posted. The disappearance of the sentinel had overcome the guards with surprise; they had gone to arouse the captain, and after a careful examination of the place, they concluded that it must be a case of desertion. Hiding in the shade, Étienne recollected this republican captain of whom the little soldier had spoken. Who knows if he might not be persuaded to pass over to the people's side! The troop would raise their rifles, and that would be the signal for a massacre of the bourgeois. A new dream took possession of him; he thought no more of dying, but remained for hours with his feet in the mud, and a drizzle from the thaw falling on his shoulders, filled by the feverish hope that victory was still possible.

Up to five o'clock he watched for the Borains. Then he perceived that the Company had cunningly arranged that they should sleep at the Voreux. The descent had begun, and the few strikers from the Deux-Cent-Quarante settlement who had been posted as scouts had not yet warned their mates. It was he who told them of the trick, and they set out running, while he waited behind the pit-bank, on the towing-path. Six o'clock struck, and the earthy sky was growing pale and lighting up with a reddish dawn, when the Abbé Ranvier came along a path, holding up his cassock above his thin legs. Every Monday he went to say an early mass at a convent chapel on the other side of the pit.

"Good morning, my friend," he shouted in a loud voice, after staring at the young man with his flaming eyes.

But Étienne did not reply. Far away between the Voreux platforms he had just seen a woman pass, and he rushed forward anxiously, for he thought he recognized Catherine. Since midnight, Catherine had been walking about the thawing roads. Chaval, on coming back and finding her in bed, had knocked her out with a blow. He shouted to her to go at once by the door if she did not wish to go by the window; and scarcely dressed, in tears, and bruised by kicks in her legs, she had been obliged to go down, pushed outside by a final thrust. This sudden separation dazed her, and she sat down on a stone, looking up at the house, still expecting that he would call her back. It was not possible; he would surely look for her and tell her to come back when he saw her thus shivering and abandoned, with no one to take her in.

At the end of two hours she made up her mind, dying of cold and as motionless as a dog thrown into the street. She left Montsou, then retraced her steps, but dared neither to call from the pathway nor to knock at the door. At last she went off by the main road to the right with the idea of going to the settlement, to her parents' house. But when she reached it she was seized by such shame that she rushed away along the gardens for fear of being recognized by someone, in spite of the heavy sleep which weighed on all eyes behind the closed shutters. And after that she wandered about, frightened at the slightest noise, trembling lest she should be seized and led away as a strumpet to that house at Marchiennes, the threat of which had haunted her like nightmare for months. Twice she stumbled against the Voreux, but terrified at the loud voices of the guard, she ran away out of breath, looking behind her to see if she was being pursued. The Réquillart lane was always full of drunken men; she went back to it, however, with the vague hope of meeting there him she had repelled a few hours earlier.

Chaval had to go down that morning, and this thought brought Catherine again towards the pit, though she felt that it would be useless to speak to him: all was over between them. There was no work going on at Jean-Bart, and he had sworn to kill her if she worked again at the Voreux, where he feared that she would compromise him, So what was to be done? – to go elsewhere, to die of hunger, to yield beneath the blows of every man who might pass? She dragged herself along, tottering amid the ruts, with aching legs and mud up to her spine. The thaw had now filled the streets with a flood of mire. She waded through it, still walking, not daring to look for a stone to sit on.

Day appeared. Catherine had just recognized the back of Chaval, who was cautiously going round the pit-bank, when she noticed Lydie and Bébert putting their noses out of their hiding-place beneath the wood supply. They had passed the night there in ambush, without going home, since Jeanlin's order was to await him; and while this latter was sleeping off the drunkenness of his murder at

Réquillart, the two children were lying in each other's arms to keep warm. The wind blew between the planks of chestnut and oak, and they rolled themselves up as in some wood-cutter's abandoned hut. Lydie did not dare to speak aloud the sufferings of a small beaten woman, any more than Bébert found courage to complain of the captain's blows which made his cheeks swell; but the captain was really abusing his power, risking their bones in mad marauding expeditions while refusing to share the booty. Their hearts rose in revolt, and they had at last embraced each other in spite of his orders, careless of that box of the ears from the invisible with which he had threatened them. It never came, so they went on kissing each other softly, with no idea of anything else, putting into that caress the passion they had long struggled against – the whole of their martyred and tender natures. All night through they had thus kept each other warm, so happy, at the bottom of this secret hole, that they could not remember that they had ever been so happy before – not even on St. Barbara's day, when they had eaten fritters and drunk wine.

The sudden sound of a bugle made Catherine start. She raised herself, and saw the Voreux guards taking up their arms. Étienne arrived running; Bébert and Lydie jumped out of their hiding-place with a. leap. And over there, beneath the growing daylight, a band of men and women were coming from the settlement, gesticulating wildly with anger.

Chapter 5

ALL the entrances to the Voreux had been closed, and the sixty soldiers, with grounded arms, were barring the only door left free, that leading to the receiving-room by a narrow staircase into which opened the captains' room and the shed. The men had been drawn up in two lines against the brick wall, so that they could not be attacked from behind.

At first the band of miners from the settlement kept at a distance. They were some thirty at most, and talked together in a violent and confused way.

Maheude, who had arrived first with dishevelled hair beneath a handkerchief knotted on in haste, and having Estelle asleep in her arms, repeated in feverish tones:

"Don't let any one in or any one out! Shut them all in there!"

Maheu approved, and just then Father Mouque arrived from Réquillart. They wanted to prevent him from passing. But he protested; he said that his horses ate their hay all the same, and cared precious little about a revolution. Besides, there was a horse dead, and they were waiting for him to draw it up. Étienne freed the old groom, and the soldiers allowed him to go to the shaft. A quarter of an hour later, as the band of strikers, which had gradually enlarged, was becoming threatening, a large door opened on the ground floor and some men appeared drawing out the dead beast, a miserable mass of flesh still fastened in the rope net; they left it in the midst of the puddles of melting snow. The surprise was so great that no one prevented the men from returning and barricading the door afresh. They all recognized the horse, with his head bent back and stiff against the plank. Whispers ran around:

"It's Trompette, isn't it? it's Trompette."

It was, in fact, Trompette. Since his descent he had never become acclimatized. He remained melancholy, with no taste for his task, as though tortured by regret for the light. In vain Bataille, the doyen of the mine, would rub him with his ribs in his friendly way, softly biting his neck to impart to him a little of the resignation gained in his ten years beneath the earth. These caresses increased his melancholy, his skin quivered beneath the confidences of the comrade who had grown old in darkness; and both of them, whenever they met and snorted together, seemed to be grieving, the old one that he could no longer remember, the young one that he could not forget. At the stable they were neighbours at the manger, and lived with lowered heads, breathing in each other's nostrils, exchanging a constant dream of daylight, visions of green grass, of white roads, of infinite yellow light. Then, when Trompette, bathed in sweat, lay in agony in his litter, Bataille had smelled at him despairingly with short sniffs like sobs. He felt that he was growing cold, the mine was taking from him his last joy, that friend fallen from above, fresh with good odours, who recalled to him his youth in the open air. And he had broken his tether, neighing with fear, when he perceived that the other no longer stirred.

Mouque had indeed warned the head captain a week ago. But much they troubled about a sick horse at such time as this! These gentlemen did not at all like moving the horses. Now, however, they had to make up their minds to take him out. The evening before the groom had spent an hour with two men tying up Trompette. They harnessed Bataille to bring him to the shaft. The old horse slowly pulled, dragging his dead comrade through so narrow a gallery that he could only shake himself at the risk of taking the skin off. And he tossed his head, listening to the grazing sound of the carcass as it went to the knacker's yard. At the pit-eye, when he was unharnessed, he followed with his melancholy eye the preparations for the ascent – the body pushed on to the cross-bars over the sump, the net fastened beneath a cage. At last the porters rang meat; he lifted his neck to see it go up, at first softly, then at once lost in the darkness, flown up for ever to the top of that black hole. And he remained with neck stretched out, his vague beast's memory perhaps recalling the things of the earth. But it was all over; he would never see his comrade again, and he himself would thus be tied up in a pitiful bundle on the day when he would ascend up there. His legs began to tremble, the fresh air which came from the distant country choked him, and he seemed intoxicated when he went heavily back to the stable.

At the surface the colliers stood gloomily before Trompette's carcass. A woman said in a low voice:

"Another man; that may go down if it likes!"

But a new flood arrived from the settlement, and Levaque, who was at the head followed by his wife and Bouteloup, shouted:

"Kill them, those Borains! No black-legs here! Kill them! Kill them!"

All rushed forward, and Étienne had to stop them. He went up to the captain, a tall thin young man of scarcely twenty-eight years, with a despairing, resolute face. He explained things to him; he tried to win him over, watching the effect of his words. What was the good of risking a useless massacre? Was not justice on the side of the miners? They were all brothers, and they ought to under-stand one another. When he came to use the world "republic" the captain made a nervous movement; but he preserved his military stiffness, and said suddenly:

"Keep off! Do not force me to do my duty."

Three times over Étienne tried again. Behind him his mates were growling. The report ran that M. Hennebeau was at the pit, and they talked of letting him down by the neck, to see if he would hew his coal himself. But it was a false report; only Négrel and Dansaert were there. They both showed themselves for a moment at a window of the receiving-room; the head captain stood in the background, rather out of countenance since his adventure with Pierronne, while the engineer bravely looked round on the crowd with his bright little eyes, smiling with that sneering contempt in which he enveloped men and things generally. Hooting arose, and they disappeared. And in their place only Souvarine's pale face was seen. He was just then on duty; he had not left his engine for a single day since the strike began, no longer talking, more and more absorbed by a fixed idea, which seemed to be shining like steel in the depths of his pale eyes.

"Keep off!" repeated the captain loudly. "I wish to hear nothing. My orders are to guard the pit, and I shall guard it. And do not press on to my men, or I shall know how to drive you back."

In spite of his firm voice, he was growing pale with increasing anxiety, as the flood of miners continued to swell. He would be relieved at midday; but fearing that he would not be able to hold out until then, he had sent a trammer from the pit to Montsou to ask for reinforcements.

Shouts had replied to him:

"Kill the blacklegs! Kill the Borains! We mean to be masters in our own place!"

Étienne drew back in despair. The end had come; there was nothing more except to fight and to die. And he ceased to hold back his mates. The mob moved up to the little troop. There were nearly four hundred of them, and the people from the neighbouring settlements were all running up. They all shouted the same cry. Maheu and Levaque said furiously to the soldiers:

"Get off with you! We have nothing against you! Get off with you!"

"This doesn't concern you," said Maheude. "Let us attend to our own affairs."

And from behind, the Levaque woman added, more violently:

"Must we eat you to get through? Just clear out of the bloody place!"

Even Lydie's shrill voice was heard. She had crammed herself in more closely, with Bébert, and was saying, in a high voice:

"Oh, the white-livered pigs!"

Catherine, a few paces off, was gazing and listening, stupefied by new scenes of violence, into the midst of which ill luck seemed to be always throwing her. Had she not suffered too much already? What fault had she committed, then, that misfortune would never give her any rest? The day before she had understood nothing of the fury of the strike; she thought that when one has one's share of blows it is useless to go and seek for more. And now her heart was swelling with hatred; she remembered what Étienne had often told her when they used to sit up; she tried to hear what he was now saying to the soldiers. He was treating them as mates; he reminded them that they also belonged to the people, and that they ought to be on the side of the people against those who took advantage of their wretchedness.

But a tremor ran through the crowd, and an old woman rushed up. It was Mother Brulé, terrible in her leanness, with her neck and arms in the air, coming up at such a pace that the wisps of her grey hair blinded her.

"Ah! by God! here I am," she stammered, out of breath; "that traitor Pierron, who shut me up in the cellar!"

And without waiting she fell on the soldiers, her black mouth belching abuse.

"Pack of scoundrels! dirty scum! ready to lick their masters' boots, and only brave against poor people!"

Then the others joined her, and there were volleys of insults. A few, indeed, cried: "Hurrah for the soldiers! to the shaft with the officer!" but soon there was only one clamour: "Down with the red-breeches!" These men, who had listened quietly, with motionless mute faces, to the fraternal appeals and the friendly attempts to win them over, preserved the same stiff passivity beneath this hail of abuse. Behind them the captain had drawn his sword, and as the crowd pressed in on them more and more, threatening to crush them against the wall, he ordered them to present bayonets. They obeyed, and a double row of steel points was placed in front of the strikers' breasts.

"Ah! the bloody swine!" yelled Mother Brulé, drawing back.

But already they were coming on again, in excited contempt of death. The women were throwing themselves forward, Maheude and the Levaque shouting:

"Kill us! Kill us, then! We want our rights!"

Levaque, at the risk of getting cut, had seized three bayonets in his hands, shaking and pulling them in the effort to snatch them away. He twisted them in the strength of his fury; while Bouteloup, standing aside, and annoyed at having followed his mate, quietly watched him.

"Just come and look here," said Maheu; "just look a bit if you are good chaps!"

And he opened his jacket and drew aside his shirt, showing his naked breast, with his hairy skin tattooed by coal. He pressed on the bayonets, compelling the soldiers to draw back, terrible in his insolence and bravado. One of them had pricked him in the chest, and he became like a madman, trying to make it enter deeper and to hear his ribs crack.

"Cowards, you don't dare! There are ten thousand behind us. Yes, you can kill us;

there are ten thousand more of us to kill yet."

The position of the soldiers was becoming critical, for they had received strict orders not to make use of their weapons until the last extremity. And how were they to prevent these furious people from impaling themselves? Besides, the space was getting less; they were now pushed back against the wall, and it was impossible to draw further back. Their little troop – a mere handful of men – opposed to the rising flood of miners, still held its own, however, and calmly executed the brief orders given by the captain. The latter, with keen eyes and nervously compressed lips, only feared lest they should be carried away by this abuse. Already a young sergeant, a tall lean fellow whose thin moustache was bristling up, was blinking his eyes in a disquieting manner. Near him an old soldier, with tanned skin and stripes won in twenty campaigns, had grown pale when he saw his bayonet twisted like a straw. Another, doubtless a recruit still smelling the fields, became very red every time he heard himself called "scum" and "riff-raff." And the violence did not cease, the outstretched fists, the abominable words, the shovelfuls of accusations and threats which buffeted their faces. It required all the force of order to keep them thus, with mute faces, in the proud, gloomy silence of military discipline.

A collision seemed inevitable, when Captain Richomme appeared from behind the troop with his benevolent white head, overwhelmed by emotion. He spoke out loudly:

"By God! this is idiotic! such tomfoolery can't go on!" And he threw himself between the bayonets and the miners.

"Mates, listen to me. You know that I am an old workman, and that I have always been one of you. Well, by God! I promise you, that if they're not just with you, I'm the man to go and say to the bosses how things lie. But this is too much, it does no good at all to howl bad names at these good fellows, and try and get your bellies ripped up."

They listened, hesitating. But up above, unfortunately, little Négrel's short profile reappeared. He feared, no doubt, that he would be accused of sending a captain in place of venturing out himself; and he tried to speak. But his voice was lost in the midst of so frightful a tumult that he had to leave the window again, simply shrugging his shoulders. Richomme then found it vain to entreat them in his own name, and to repeat that the thing must be arranged between mates; they repelled him, suspecting him. But he was obstinate and remained amongst them.

"By God! let them break my head as well as yours, for I don't leave you while you are so foolish!"

Étienne, whom he begged to help him in making them hear reason, made a gesture of powerlessness. It was too late, there were now more than five hundred of them. And besides the madmen who were rushing up to chase away the Borains, some came out of inquisitiveness, or to joke and amuse themselves over the battle. In the midst of one group, at some distance, Zacharie and Philoméne were looking on as at a theatre so peacefully that they had brought their two children, Achille and Désirée. Another stream was arriving from Réquillart, including Mouquet and Mouquette. The former at once went on, grinning, to slap his friend Zacharie on the back; while Mouquette, in a very excited condition, rushed to the first rank of the evil-disposed.

Meanwhile, every minute, the captain looked down the Montsou road. The desired reinforcements had not arrived, and his sixty men could hold out no longer. At last it occurred to him to strike the imagination of the crowd, and he ordered his men to load. The soldiers executed the order, but the disturbance increased, the blustering, and the mockery.

"Ah! these shammers, they're going off to the target!" jeered the women, the Brulé, the Levaque, and the others.

Maheude, with her breast covered by the little body of Estelle, who was awake and crying, came so near that the sergeant asked her what she was going to do with that poor little brat.

"What the devil's that to do with you?" she replied. "Fire at it if you dare!"

The men shook their heads with contempt. None believed that they would fire on them.

"There are no balls in their cartridges," said Levaque. "Are we Cossacks?" cried Maheu. "You don't fire against Frenchmen, by God!"

Others said that when people had been through the Crimean campaign they were not afraid of lead. And all continued to thrust themselves on to the rifles. If firing had begun at this moment the crowd would have been mown down.

In the front rank Mouquette was choking with fury, thinking that the soldiers were going to gash the women's skins. She had spat out all her coarse words at them, and could find no vulgarity low enough, when suddenly, having nothing left but that mortal offence with which to bombard the faces of the troop, she exhibited her backside. With both hands she raised her skirts, bent her back, and expanded the enormous rotundity.

"Here, that's for you! and it's a lot too clean, you dirty blackguards!"

She ducked and butted so that each might have his share, repeating after each thrust:

"There's for the officer! there's for the sergeant! there's for the soldiers!"

A tempest of laughter arose; Bébert and Lydie were in convulsions; Étienne himself, in spite of his sombre expectation, applauded this insulting nudity. All of them, the banterers as well as the infuriated, were now hooting the soldiers as though they had seen them stained by a splash of filth; Catherine only, standing aside on some old timber, remained silent with the blood at her heart, slowly carried away by the hatred that was rising within her.

But a hustling took place. To calm the excitement of his men, the captain decided to make prisoners. With a leap Mouquette escaped, saving herself between the legs of her comrades. Three miners, Levaque and two others, were seized among the more violent, and kept in sight at the other end of the captains' room. Négrel and Dansaert, above, were shouting to the captain to come in and take refuge with them. He refused; he felt that these buildings with their doors without locks would be carried by assault, and that he would undergo the shame of being disarmed. His little troop was already growling with impatience; it was impossible to flee before these wretches in sabots. The sixty, with their backs to the wall and their rifles loaded, again faced the mob.

At first there was a recoil, followed by deep silence; the strikers were astonished at this energetic stroke. Then a cry arose calling for the prisoners, demanding their immediate release. Some voices said that they were being murdered in there. And without any attempt at concerted action, carried away by the same impulse, by the same desire for revenge, they all ran to the piles of bricks which stood near, those bricks for which the marly soil supplied the clay, and which were baked on the spot. The children brought them one by one, and the women filled their skirts with them. Every one soon had her ammunition at her feet, and the battle of stones began.

It was Mother Brulé who set to first. She broke the bricks on the sharp edge of her knee, and with both hands she discharged the two fragments. The Levaque woman was almost putting her shoulders out, being so large and soft that she had to come near to get her aim, in spite of Bouteloup's entreaties, and he dragged her back in the hope of being able to lead her away now that her husband had been taken off. They all grew excited, and Mouquette, tired of making herself bleed by breaking the bricks on her over fat thighs, preferred to throw them whole.

Even the youngsters came into line, and Bébert showed Lydie how the brick ought to be sent from under the elbow. It was a shower of enormous hail-stones, producing low thuds. And suddenly, in the midst of these furies, Catherine was observed with her fists in the air also brandishing half-bricks and throwing them with all the force of her little arms. She could not have said why, she was suffocating, she was dying of the desire to kill everybody. Would it not soon be done with, this cursed life of misfortune? She had had enough of it, beaten and driven away by her man, wandering about like a lost dog in the mud of the roads, without being able to ask a crust from her father, who was starving like herself. Things never seemed to get better; they were getting worse ever since she could remember. And she broke the bricks and threw them before her with the one idea of sweeping everything away, her eyes so blinded that she could not even see whose jaws she might be crushing.

Étienne, who had remained in front of the soldiers, nearly had his skull broken. His ear was grazed, and turning round he started when he realized that the brick had come from Catherine's feverish hands; but at the risk of being killed he remained where he was, gazing at her. Many others also forgot themselves there, absorbed in the battle, with empty hands. Mouquet criticized the blows as though he were looking on at a game of *bouchon*. Oh, that was well struck! and that other, no luck! He joked, and with his elbow pushed Zacharie, who was squabbling with Philoméne because he had boxed Achille's and Désirée's ears, refusing to put them on his back so that they could see. There were spectators crowded all along the road. And at the top of the slope near the entrance to the settlement, old Bonnemort appeared, resting on his stick, motionless against the rust-coloured sky.

As soon as the first bricks were thrown, Captain Richomme had again placed himself between the soldiers and the miners. He was entreating the one party, exhorting the other party, careless of danger, in such despair that large tears were flowing from his eyes. It was impossible to hear his words in the midst of the tumult; only his large grey moustache could be seen moving.

But the hail of bricks came faster; the men were joining in, following the example of the women.

Then Maheude noticed that Maheu was standing behind with empty hands and sombre air.

"What's up with you?" she shouted. "Are you a coward? Are you going to let your mates be carried off to prison? Ah! if only I hadn't got this child, you should see!"

Estelle, who was clinging to her neck, screaming, prevented her from joining Mother Brulé and the others. And as her man did not seem to hear, she kicked some bricks against his legs.

"By God! will you take that? Must I spit in your face before people to get your spirits up?"

Becoming very red, he broke some bricks and threw them. She lashed him on, dazing him, shouting behind him cries of death, stifling her daughter against her breast with the spasm of her arms; and he still moved forward until he was opposite the guns.

Beneath this shower of stones the little troop was disappearing. Fortunately they struck too high, and the wall was riddled. What was to be done? The idea of going in, of turning their backs for a moment turned the captain's pale face purple; but it was no longer possible, they would be torn to pieces at the least movement. A brick had just broken the peak of his cap, drops of blood were running down his forehead. Several of his men were wounded; and he felt that they were losing self-control in that unbridled instinct of self-defence when obedience to leaders ceases. The sergeant had uttered a "By God!" for his left shoulder had nearly been put out, and his flesh bruised by a shock like the blow of a washer-woman's beetle against linen. Grazed twice over, the recruit had his thumb smashed, while his right knee was grazed. Were they to let themselves be worried much longer? A stone having bounded back and struck the old soldier with the stripes beneath the belly, his cheeks turned green, and his weapon trembled as he stretched it out at the end of his lean arms. Three times the captain was on the point of ordering them to fire. He was choked by anguish; an endless struggle for several seconds set at odds in his mind all ideas and duties, all his beliefs as a man and as a soldier. The rain of bricks increased, and he opened his mouth and was about to shout "Fire!" when the guns went off of themselves three shots at first, then five, then the roll of a volley, then one by itself, some time afterwards, in the deep silence.

There was stupefaction on all sides. They had fired, and the gaping crowd stood motionless, as yet unable to believe it. But heart-rending cries arose while the bugle was sounding to cease firing. And here was a mad panic, the rush of cattle filled with grapeshot, a wild flight through the mud. Bébert and Lydie had fallen one on top of the other at the first three shots, the little girl struck in the face, the boy wounded beneath the left shoulder. She was crushed, and never stirred again. But he moved, seized her with both arms in the convulsion of his agony, as if he wanted to take her again, as he had taken her at the bottom of the black hiding-place where they had spent the past night. And Jeanlin, who just then ran up from Réquillart still half asleep, kicking about in the midst of the smoke, saw him embrace his little wife and die.

The five other shots had brought down Mother Brulé and Captain Richomme. Struck in the back as he was entreating his mates, he had fallen on to his knees, and slipping on to one hip he was groaning on the ground with eyes still full of tears. The old woman, whose breast had been opened, had fallen back stiff and crackling, like a bundle of dry faggots, stammering one last oath in the gurgling of blood.

But then the volley swept the field, mowing down the inquisitive groups who were laughing at the battle a hundred paces off. A ball entered Mouquet's mouth and threw him down with fractured skull at the feet of Zacharie and Philoméne, whose two youngsters were splashed with red drops. At the same moment Mouquette received two balls in the belly. She had seen the soldiers take aim, and in an instinctive movement of her good nature she had thrown herself in front of Catherine, shouting out to her to take care; she uttered a loud cry and fell on to her back overturned by the shock. Étienne ran up, wishing to raise her and take her away; but with a gesture she said it was all over. Then she groaned, but without ceasing to smile at both of them, as though she were glad to see them together now that she was going away.

All seemed to be over, and the hurricane of balls was lost in the distance as far as the frontages of the settlement, when the last shot, isolated and delayed, was fired. Maheu, struck in the heart, turned round and fell with his face down into a puddle black with coal. Maheude leant down in stupefaction.

"Eh! old man, get up. It's nothing, is it?"

Her hands were engaged with Estelle, whom she had to put under one arm in order to turn her man's head.

"Say something! where are you hurt?"

His eyes were vacant, and his mouth was slavered with bloody foam. She understood: he was dead. Then she remained seated in the mud with her daughter under her arm like a bundle, gazing at her old man with a besotted air.

The pit was free. With a nervous movement the captain had taken off and then put on his cap, struck by a stone; he preserved his pallid stiffness in face of the disaster of his life, while his men with mute faces were reloading. The frightened faces of Négrel and Dansaert could be seen at the window of the receiving-room. Souvarine was behind them with a deep wrinkle on his forehead, as though the nail of his fixed idea had printed itself there threateningly. On the other side of the horizon, at the edge of the plain,

Bonnemort had not moved, supported by one hand on his stick, the other hand up to his brows to see better the murder of his people below. The wounded were howling, the dead were growing cold. in twisted postures, muddy with the liquid mud of the thaw, here and there forming puddles among the inky patches of coal which reappeared beneath the tattered snow. And in the midst of these human corpses, all small, poor and lean in their wretchedness, lay Trompette's carcass, a monstrous and pitiful mass of dead flesh.

Étienne had not been killed. He was still waiting beside Catherine, who had fallen from fatigue and anguish, when a sonorous voice made him start. It was Abbé Ranvier, who was coming back after saying mass, and who, with both arms in the air, with the inspired fury of a prophet, was calling the wrath of God down on the murderers. He foretold the era of justice, the approaching extermination of the middle class by fire from heaven, since it was bringing its crimes to a climax by massacring the workers and the disinherited of the world.

Part 7

Chapter 1

THE shots fired at Montsou had reached as far as Paris with a formidable echo. For four days all the opposition journals had been indignant, displaying atrocious narratives on their front pages: twenty-five wounded, fourteen dead, including three women and two children. And there were prisoners taken as well; Levaque had become a sort of hero, and was credited with a reply of antique sublimity to the examining magistrate. The empire, hit in mid career by these few balls, affected the calm of omnipotence, without itself realizing the gravity of its wound. It was simply an unfortunate collision, something lost over there in the black country, very far from the Parisian boulevards which formed public opinion; it would soon be forgotten. The Company had received official intimation to hush up the affair, and to put an end to a strike which from its irritating duration was becoming a social danger.

So on Wednesday morning three of the directors appeared at Montsou. The little town, sick at heart, which had not dared hitherto to rejoice over the massacre, now breathed again, and tasted the joy of being saved. The weather, too, had become fine; there was a bright sun – one of those first February days which, with their moist warmth, tip the lilac shoots with green. All the shutters had been flung back at the administration building, the vast structure seemed alive again. And cheering rumours were circulating; it was said that the directors, deeply affected by the catastrophe, had rushed down to open their paternal arms to the wanderers from the settlements. Now that the blow had fallen – a more vigorous one doubtless than they had wished for – they were prodigal in their task of relief, and decreed measures that were excellent though tardy. First of all they sent away the Borains, and made much of this extreme concession to their workmen. Then they put an end to the military occupation of the pits, which were no longer threatened by the crushed strikers. They also obtained silence regarding the sentinel who had disappeared from the Voreux; the district had been searched without finding either the gun or the corpse, and although there was a suspicion of crime, it was decided to consider the soldier a deserter. In every way they thus tried to attenuate matters, trembling with fear for the morrow, judging it dangerous to acknowledge the irresistible savagery of a crowd set free amid the falling structure of the old world. And besides, this work of conciliation did not prevent them from bringing purely administrative affairs to a satisfactory conclusion; for Deneulin had been seen to return to the administration buildings, where he met M. Hennebeau. The negotiations for the purchase of Vandame continued, and it was considered certain that Deneulin would accept the Company's offers.

But what particularly stirred the country were the great yellow posters which the directors had stuck up in profusion on the walls. On them were to be read these few lines, in very large letters: "Workers of Montsou! We do not wish that the errors of which you have lately seen the sad effects should deprive sensible and willing workmen of their livelihood. We shall therefore reopen all the pits on Monday morning, and when work is resumed we shall examine with care and consideration those cases in which there may be room for improvement. We shall, in fact, do all that is just or possible to do." In one morning the ten thousand colliers passed before these placards. Not one of them spoke, many shook their heads, others went away with trailing steps, without changing one line in their motionless faces.

Up till now the settlement of the Deux-Cent-Quarante had persisted in its fierce resistance. It seemed that the blood of their mates, which had reddened the mud of the pit, was barricading the road against the others. Scarcely a dozen had gone down, merely Pierron and some sneaks of his sort, whose departure and arrival were gloomily watched without a gesture or a threat. Therefore a deep suspicion greeted the placard stuck on to the church. Nothing was said about the returned certificates in that. Would the Company refuse to take them on again? and the fear of retaliations, the fraternal idea of protesting against the dismissal of the more compromised men, made them all obstinate still. It was dubious; they would see. They would return to the pit when these gentlemen were good enough to put things plainly. Silence crushed the low houses. Hunger itself seemed nothing; all might die now that violent death had passed over their roofs.

But one house, that of the Maheus, remained especially black and mute in its overwhelming grief. Since she had followed her man to the cemetery, Maheude kept her teeth clenched. After the battle, she had allowed Étienne to bring back Catherine muddy and half dead; and as she was undressing her, before the young man, in order to put her to bed, she thought for a moment that her daughter also had received a ball in the belly, for the chemise was marked with large patches of blood. But she soon understood that it was the flood of puberty, which was at last breaking out in the shock of this abominable day. Ah! another piece of luck, that wound! A fine present, to be able to make children for the gendarmes to kill; and she never spoke to Catherine, nor did she, indeed, talk to Étienne. The latter slept with Jeanlin, at the risk of being arrested, seized by such horror at the idea of going back to the darkness of Réquillart that he would have preferred a prison. A shudder shook him, the horror of the night after all those deaths, an unacknowledged fear of the little soldier who slept down there underneath the rocks. Besides, he dreamed of a prison as of a refuge in the midst of the torment of his defeat; but they did not trouble him, and he dragged on his wretched hours, not knowing how to weary out his body. Only at times Maheude looked at both of them, at him and her daughter, with a spiteful air, as though she were asking them what they were doing in her house.

Once more they were all snoring in a heap. Father Bonnemort occupied the former bed of the two youngsters, who slept with Catherine now that poor Alzire no longer dug her hump into her big sister's ribs. It was when going to bed that the mother felt the emptiness of the house by the coldness of her bed, which was now too large. In vain she took Estelle to fill the vacancy; that did not replace her man, and she wept quietly for hours. Then the days began to pass by as before, always without bread, but without the luck to die outright; things picked up here and there rendered to the wretches the poor service of keeping them alive. Nothing had changed in their existence, only her man was gone.

On the afternoon of the fifth day, Étienne, made miserable by the sight of this silent woman, left the room, and walked slowly along the paved street of the settlement. The inaction which weighed on him impelled him to take constant walks, with arms swinging idly and lowered head, always tortured by the same thought. He tramped thus for half an hour, when he felt, by an increase in his discomfort, that his mates were coming to their doors to look at him. His little remaining popularity had been driven to the winds by that fusillade, and he never passed now without meeting fiery looks which pursued him. When he raised his head there were threatening men there, women drawing aside the curtains from their windows; and beneath this still silent accusation and the restrained anger of these eyes, enlarged by hunger and tears, he became awkward and could scarcely walk straight. These dumb reproaches seemed to be always increasing behind him. He became so terrified, lest he should hear the entire settlement come out to shout its wretchedness at him, that he returned shuddering. But at the Maheus' the scene which met him still further agitated him. Old Bonnemort was near the cold fireplace, nailed to his chair ever since two neighbours, on the day of the slaughter, had found him on the ground, with his stick broken, struck down like an old thunder-stricken tree. And while

Lénore and Henri, to beguile their hunger, were scraping, with deafening noise, an old saucepan in which cabbages had been boiled the day before, Maheude, after having placed Estelle on the table, was standing up threatening Catherine with her fist.

"Say that again, by God! Just dare to say that again!" Catherine had declared her intention to go back to the Voreux. The idea of not gaining her bread, of being thus tolerated in her mother's house, like a useless animal that is in the way, was becoming every day more unbearable; and if it had not been for the fear of Chaval she would have gone down on Tuesday.

She said again, stammering:

"What would you have? We can't go on doing nothing. We should get bread, anyhow."

Maheude interrupted her.

"Listen to me: the first one of you who goes to work, I'll do for you. No, that would be too much, to kill the father and go on taking it out of the children! I've had enough of it; I'd rather see you all put in your coffins, like him that's gone already."

And her long silence broke out into a furious flood of words. A fine sum Catherine would bring her! hardly thirty sous, to which they might add twenty sous if the bosses were good enough to find work for that brigand Jeanlin. Fifty sous, and seven mouths to feed! The brats were only good to swallow soup. As to the grandfather, he must have broken something in his brain when he fell, for he seemed imbecile; unless it had turned his blood to see the soldiers firing at his mates.

"That's it, old man, isn't it? They've quite done for you. It's no good having your hands still strong; you're done for."

Bonnemort looked at her with his dim eyes without understanding. He remained for hours with fixed gaze, having no intelligence now except to spit into a plate filled with ashes, which was put beside him for cleanliness.

"And they've not settled his pension, either," she went on. "And I'm sure they won't give it, because of our ideas. No! I tell you that we've too much to do with those people who bring ill luck."

"But," Catherine ventured to say, "they promise on the placard–"

"Just let me alone with your damned placard! More bird-lime for catching us and eating us. They can be mighty kind now that they have ripped us open."

"But where shall we go, mother? They won't keep us at the settlement, sure enough."

Maheude made a vague, terrified gesture. Where should they go to? She did not know at all; she avoided thinking, it made her mad. They would go elsewhere – somewhere. And as the noise of the saucepan was becoming unbearable, she turned round on Lénore and Henri and boxed their ears. The fall of Estelle, who had been crawling on all fours, increased the disturbance. The mother quieted her with a push – a good thing if it had killed her! She spoke of Alzire; she wished the others might have that child's luck. Then suddenly she burst out into loud sobs, with her head against the wall.

Étienne, who was standing by, did not dare to interfere. He no longer counted for anything in the house, and even the children drew back from him suspiciously. But the unfortunate woman's tears went to his heart, and he murmured:

"Come, come! courage! we must try to get out of it." She did not seem to hear him, and was bemoaning herself now in a low continuous complaint.

"Ah! the wretchedness! is it possible? Things did go on before these horrors. We ate our bread dry, but we were all together; and what has happened, good God! What have we done, then, that we should have such troubles – some under the earth, and the others with nothing left but to long to get there too? It's true enough that they harnessed us like horses to work, and it's not at all a just sharing of things to be always getting the stick and making rich people's fortunes bigger without hope of ever tasting the good things. There's no pleasure in life when hope goes. Yes, that couldn't have gone on longer; we had to breathe a bit. If we had only known! Is it possible to make oneself so wretched through wanting justice?"

Sighs swelled her breast, and her voice choked with immense sadness.

"Then there are always some clever people there who promise you that everything can be arranged by just taking a little trouble. Then one loses one's head, and one suffers so much from things as they are that one asks for things that can't be. Now, I was dreaming like a fool; I seemed to see a life of good friendship with everybody; I went off into the air, my faith! into the clouds. And then one breaks one's back when one tumbles down into the mud again. It's not true; there's nothing over there of the things that people tell of. What there is, is only wretchedness, ah! wretchedness, as much as you like of it, and bullets into the bargain."

Étienne listened to this lamentation, and every tear struck him with remorse. He knew not what to say to calm Maheude, broken by her terrible fall from the heights of the ideal. She had come back to the middle of the room, and was now looking at him; she addressed him with contemptuous familiarity in a last cry of rage:

"And you, do you talk of going back to the pit, too, after driving us out of the bloody place! I've nothing to reproach you with; but if I were in your shoes I should be dead of grief by now after causing such harm to the mates."

He was about to reply, but then shrugged his shoulders in despair. What was the good of explaining, for she would not understand in her grief?

And he went away, for he was suffering too much, and resumed his wild walk outside.

There again he found the settlement apparently waiting for him, the men at the doors, the women at the windows. As soon as he appeared growls were heard, and the crowd increased. The breath of gossip, which had been swelling for four days, was breaking out in a universal malediction. Fists were stretched towards him, mothers spitefully pointed him out to their boys, old men spat as they looked at him. It was the change which follows on the morrow of defeat, the fatal reverse of popularity, an execration exasperated by all the suffering endured without result. He had to pay for famine and death.

Zacharie, who came up with Philoméne, hustled Étienne as he went out, grinning maliciously.

"Well, he gets fat. It's filling, then, to live on other people's deaths?"

The Levaque woman had already come to her door with Bouteloup. She spoke of Bébert, her youngster, killed by a bullet, and cried:

"Yes, there are cowards who get children murdered! Let him go and look for mine in the earth if he wants to give it me back!"

She was forgetting her man in prison, for the household was going on since Bouteloup remained; but she thought of him, however, and went on in a shrill voice:

"Get along! rascals may walk about while good people are put away!"

In avoiding her, Étienne tumbled on to Pierrone, who was running up across the gardens. She had regarded her mother's death as a deliverance, for the old woman's violence threatened to get them hanged; nor did she weep over Pierron's little girl, that street-walker Lydie – a good riddance. But she joined in with her neighbours with the idea of getting reconciled with them.

"And my mother, eh, and the little girl? You were seen; you were hiding yourself behind them when they caught the lead instead of you!"

What was to be done? Strangle Pierronne and the others, and fight the whole settlement? Étienne wanted to do so for a moment. The blood was throbbing in his head, he now looked upon his mates as brutes, he was irritated to see them so unintelligent and barbarous that they wanted to revenge themselves on him for the logic of facts. How stupid it all was! and he felt disgust at his powerlessness to tame them again; and satisfied himself with hastening his steps as though he were deaf to abuse. Soon it became a flight; every house hooted him as he passed, they hastened on his heels, it was a whole nation cursing him with a voice that was becoming like thunder in its overwhelming hatred. It was he, the exploiter, the murderer, who was the sole cause of their misfortune. He rushed out of the settlement, pale and terrified, with this yelling crowd behind his back. When he at last reached the main road most of them left him; but a few persisted, until at the bottom of the slope before the Avantage he met another group coming from the Voreux.

Old Mouque and Chaval were there. Since the death of his daughter Mouquette, and of his son Mouquet, the old man had continued to act as groom without a word of regret or complaint. Suddenly, when he saw Étienne, he was shaken by fury, tears broke out from his eyes, and a flood of coarse words burst from his mouth, black and bleeding from his habit of chewing tobacco.

"You devil! you bloody swine! you filthy snout! Wait, you've got to pay me for my poor children; you'll have to come to it!"

He picked up a brick, broke it, and threw both pieces. "Yes! yes! clear him off!"

shouted Chaval, who was grinning in excitement, delighted at this vengeance. "Every one gets his turn; now you're up against the wall, you dirty hound!"

And he also attacked Étienne with stones. A savage clamour arose; they all took up bricks, broke them, and threw them, to rip him open, as they would like to have done to the soldiers. He was dazed and could not flee; he faced them, trying to calm them with phrases. His old speeches, once so warmly received, came back to his lips. He repeated the words with which he had intoxicated them at the time when he could keep them in hand like a faithful flock; but his power was dead, and only stones replied to him. He had just been struck on the left arm, and was drawing back, in great peril, when he found himself hemmed in against the front of the Avantage.

For the last few moments Rasseneur had been at his door.

"Come in," he said simply.

Étienne hesitated; it choked him to take refuge there.

"Come in; then I'll speak to them."

He resigned himself, and took refuge at the other end of the parlour, while the innkeeper filled up the doorway with his broad shoulders.

"Look here, my friends, just be reasonable. You know very well that I've never deceived you. I've always been in favour of quietness, and if you had listened to me, you certainly wouldn't be where you are now."

Rolling his shoulders and belly, he went on at length, allowing his facile eloquence to flow with the lulling gentleness of warm water. And all his old success came back; he regained his popularity, naturally and without an effort, as if he had never been hooted and called a coward a month before. Voices arose in approval: "Very good! we are with you! that is the way to put it!" Thundering applause broke out.

Étienne, in the background, grew faint, and there was bitterness at his heart. He recalled Rasseneur's prediction in the forest, threatening him with the ingratitude of the mob. What imbecile brutality! What an abominable forgetfulness of old services! It was a blind force which constantly devoured itself. And beneath his anger at seeing these brutes spoil their own cause, there was despair at his own fall and the tragic end of his ambition. What! was it already done for! He remembered hearing beneath the beeches three thousand hearts beating to the echo of his own. On that day he had held his popularity in both hands. Those people belonged to him; he felt that he was their master. Mad dreams had then intoxicated him. Montsou at his feet, Paris beyond, becoming a deputy perhaps, crushing the middle class in a speech, the first speech ever pronounced by a workman in a parliament. And it was all over! He awakened, miserable and detested; his people were dismissing him by flinging bricks.

Rasseneur's voice rose higher:

"Never will violence succeed; the world can't be re-made in a day. Those who have promised you to change it all at one stroke are either making fun of you or they are rascals!"

"Bravo! bravo!" shouted the crowd.

Who then was the guilty one? And this question which Étienne put to himself overwhelmed him more than ever. Was it in fact his fault, this misfortune which was making him bleed, the wretchedness of some, the murder of others, these women, these children, lean, and without bread? He had had that lamentable vision one evening before the catastrophe. But then a force was lifting him, he was carried away with his mates. Besides, he had never led them, it was they who led him, who obliged him to do things which he would never have done if it were not for the shock of that crowd pushing behind him. At each new violence he had been stupefied by the course of events, for he had neither foreseen nor desired any of them. Could he anticipate, for instance, that his followers in the settlement would one day stone him? These infuriated people lied when they accused him of having promised them an existence all fodder and laziness. And in this justification, in this reasoning, in which he tried to fight against his remorse, was hidden the anxiety that he had not risen to the height of his task; it was the doubt of the half-cultured man still perplexing him. But he felt himself at the end of his courage, he was no longer at heart with his mates; he feared this enormous mass of the people, blind and irresistible, moving like a force of nature, sweeping away everything, outside rules and theories. A certain repugnance was detaching him from them – the discomfort of his new tastes, the slow movement of all his being towards a superior class.

At this moment Rasseneur's voice was lost in the midst of enthusiastic shouts:

"Hurrah for Rasseneur! he's the fellow! Bravo, bravo!"

The innkeeper shut the door, while the band dispersed; and the two men looked at each other in silence. They both shrugged their shoulders. They finished up by having a drink together.

On the same day there was a great dinner at Piolaine; they were celebrating the betrothal of Négrel and Cécile. Since the previous evening the Grégoires had had the dining-room waxed and the drawing-room dusted. Mélanie reigned in the kitchen, watching over the roasts and stirring the sauces, the odour of which ascended to the attics. It had been decided that Francis, the coachman, should help Honorine to wait. The gardener's wife would wash up, and the gardener would open the gate. Never had the substantial, patriarchal old house been in such a state of gaiety.

Everything went off beautifully, Madame Hennebeau was charming with Cécile, and she smiled at Négrel when the Montsou lawyer gallantly proposed the health of the future household. M. Hennebeau was also very amiable. His smiling face struck the guests. The report circulated that he was rising in favour with the directors, and that he would soon be made an officer of the Legion of Honour, on account of the energetic manner in which he had put down the strike. Nothing was said about recent events; but there was an air of triumph in the general joy, and the dinner became the official celebration of a victory. At last, then, they were saved, and once more they could begin to eat and sleep in peace. A discreet allusion was made to those dead whose blood the Voreux mud had yet scarcely drunk up. It was a necessary lesson: and they were all affected when the Grégoires added that it was now the duty of all to go and heal the wounds in the settlements. They had regained their benevolent placidity, excusing their brave miners, whom they could already see again at the bottom of the mines, giving a good example of everlasting resignation. The Montsou notables, who had now left off trembling, agreed that this question of the wage system ought to be studied, cautiously. The roasts came on; and the victory became complete when M. Hennebeau read a letter from the bishop announcing Abbé Ranvier's removal. The middle class throughout the province had been roused to anger by the story of this priest who treated the soldiers as murderers. And when the dessert appeared the lawyer resolutely declared that he was a free-thinker. Deneulin was there with his two daughters. In the midst of the joy, he forced himself to hide the melancholy of his ruin. That very morning he had signed the sale of his Vandame concession to the Montsou Company. With the knife at his throat he had submitted to the directors' demands, at last giving up to them that prey they had been on the watch for so long, scarcely obtaining from them the money necessary to pay off his creditors. He had even accepted, as a lucky chance, at the last moment, their offer to keep him as divisional engineer, thus resigning himself to watch, as a simple salaried servant, over that pit which had swallowed up his fortune. It was the knell of small personal enterprises, the approaching disappearance of the masters, eaten up, one by one, by the ever-hungry ogre of capital, drowned in the rising flood of great companies. He alone paid the expenses of the strike; he understood that they were drinking to his disaster when they drank to M. Hennebeau's rosette. And he only consoled himself a little when he saw the fine courage of Lucie and Jeanne, who looked charming in their done-up toilettes, laughing at the downfall, like happy tomboys disdainful of money.

When they passed into the drawing-room for coffee, M. Grégoire drew his cousin aside and congratulated him on the courage of his decision.

"What would you have? Your real mistake was to risk the million of your Montsou denier over Vandame. You gave yourself a terrible wound, and it has melted away in that dog's labour, while mine, which has not stirred from my drawer, still keeps me comfortably doing nothing, as it will keep my grandchildren's children."

Chapter 2

ON Sunday Étienne escaped from the settlement at nightfall. A very clear sky, sprinkled with stars, lit up the earth with the blue haze of twilight. He went down towards the canal, and followed the bank slowly, in the direction of Marchiennes. It was his favourite walk, a grass-covered path two leagues long, passing straight beside this geometrical water-way, which unrolled itself like an endless ingot of molten silver. He never met any one there. But on this day he was vexed to see a man come up to him. Beneath the pale starlight, the two solitary walkers only recognized each other when they were face to face.

"What! is it you?" said Étienne.

Souvarine nodded his head without replying. For a moment they remained motionless, then side by side they set out towards Marchiennes. Each of them seemed to be continuing his own reflections, as though they were far away from each other.

"Have you seen in the paper about Pluchart's success at Paris?" asked Étienne, at length. "After that meeting at Belleville, they waited for him on the pavement, and gave him an ovation. Oh! he's afloat now, in spite of his sore throat. He can do what he likes in the future."

The engine-man shrugged his shoulders. He felt contempt for fine talkers, fellows who go into politics as one goes to the bar, to get an income out of phrases.

Étienne was now studying Darwin. He had read fragments, summarized and popularized in a five-sou volume; and out of this ill-understood reading he had gained for himself a revolutionary idea of the struggle for existence, the lean eating the fat, the strong people devouring the pallid middle class. But Souvarine furiously attacked the stupidity of the Socialists who accept

Darwin, that apostle of scientific inequality, whose famous selection was only good for aristocratic philosophers. His mate persisted, however, wishing to reason out the matter, and expressing his doubts by an hypothesis: supposing the old society were no longer to exist, swept away to the crumbs; well, was it not to be feared that the new world would grow up again, slowly spoilt by the same injustices, some sick and others flourishing, some more skilful and intelligent, fattening on everything, and others imbecile and lazy. becoming slaves again? But before this vision of eternal wretchedness, the engine-man shouted out fiercely that if justice was not possible with man, then man must disappear. For every rotten society there must be a massacre, until the last creature was exterminated. And there was silence again.

For a long time, with sunken head, Souvarine walked over the short grass, so absorbed that he kept to the extreme edge, by the water, with the quiet certainty of a sleep-walker on a roof. Then he shuddered causelessly, as though he had stumbled against a shadow. His eyes lifted and his face was very pale; he said softly to his companion:

"Did I ever tell you how she died?"

"Whom do you mean?"

"My woman, over there, in Russia."

Étienne made a vague gesture, astonished at the tremor in his voice and at the sudden desire for confidence in this lad, who was usually so impassive in his stoical detachment from others and from himself. He only knew that the woman was his mistress, and that she had been hanged at Moscow.

"The affair hadn't gone off," Souvarine said, with eyes still vacantly following the white stream of the canal between the bluish colonnades of tall trees. "We had been a fortnight at the bottom of a hole undermining the railway, and it was not the imperial train that was blown up, it was a passenger train. Then they arrested

Annutchka. She brought us bread every evening, disguised as a peasant woman. She lit the fuse, too, because a man might have attracted attention. I followed the trial, hidden in the crowd, for six days."

His voice became thick, and he coughed as though he were choking.

"Twice I wanted to cry out, and to rush over the people's heads to join her. But what was the good? One man less would be one soldier less; and I could see that she was telling me not to come, when her large eyes met mine."

He coughed again.

"On the last day in the square I was there. It was raining; they stupidly lost their heads, put out by the falling rain. It took twenty minutes to hang the other four; the cord broke, they could not finish the fourth. Annutchka was standing up waiting. She could not see me, she was looking for me in the crowd. I got on to a post and she saw me, and our eyes never turned from each other. When she was dead she was still looking at me. I waved my hat; I came away."

There was silence again. The white road of the canal unrolled to the far distance, and they both walked with the same quiet step as though each had fallen back into his isolation. At the horizon, the pale water seemed to open the sky with a little hole of light.

"It was our punishment," Souvarine went on roughly. "We were guilty to love each other. Yes, it is well that she is dead; heroes will be born from her blood, and I no longer have any cowardice at my heart. Ah! nothing, neither parents, nor wife, nor friend! Nothing to make my hand tremble on the day when I must take others' lives or give up my own."

Étienne had stopped, shuddering in the cool night. He discussed no more, he simply said:

"We have gone far; shall we go back?"

They went back towards the Voreux slowly, and he added, after a few paces:

"Have you seen the new placards?"

The Company had that morning put up some more large yellow posters. They were clearer and more conciliatory, and the Company undertook to take back the certificates of those miners who went down on the following day. Everything would be forgotten, and pardon was offered even to those who were most implicated.

"Yes, I've seen," replied the engine-man.

"Well, what do you think of it?"

"I think that it's all up. The flock will go down again. You are all too cowardly."

Étienne feverishly excused his mates: a man may be brave, a mob which is dying of hunger has no strength. Step by step they were returning to the Voreux; and before the black mass of the pit he continued swearing that he, at least, would never go down; but he could forgive those who did. Then, as the rumour ran that the carpenters had not had time to repair the tubbing, he asked for information. Was it true? Had the weight of the soil against the timber which formed the internal skirt of scaffolding to the shaft so pushed it in that the winding-cages rubbed as they went down for a length of over fifty metres?

Souvarine, who once more became uncommunicative, replied briefly. He had been working the day before, and the cage did, in fact, jar; the engine-men had even had to double the speed to pass that spot. But all the bosses received any observations with the same irritating remark: it was coal they wanted; that could be repaired later on.

"You see that is smashing up!" Étienne murmured. "It will be a fine time!"

With eyes vaguely fixed on the pit in the shadow, Souvarine quietly concluded:

"If it does smash up, the mates will know it, since you advise them to go down again."

Nine o'clock struck at the Montsou steeple; and his companion having said that he was going to bed, he added, without putting out his hand:

"Well, good-bye. I'm going away."

"What! you're going away?"

"Yes, I've asked for my certificate back. I'm going elsewhere."

Étienne, stupefied and affected, looked at him. After walking for two hours he said that to him! And in so calm a voice, while the mere announcement of this sudden separation made his own heart ache. They had got to know each other, they had toiled together; that always makes one sad, the idea of not seeing a person again.

"You're going away! And where do you go?"

"Over there – I don't know at all."

"But I shall see you again?"

"No, I think not."

They were silent and remained for a moment facing each other without finding anything to say.

"Then good-bye."

"Good-bye."

While Étienne ascended toward the settlement, Souvarine turned and again went along the canal bank; and there, now alone, he continued to walk, with sunken head, so lost in the darkness that he seemed merely a moving shadow of the night. Now and then he stopped, he counted the hours that struck afar. When he heard midnight strike he left the bank and turned towards the Voreux.

At that time the pit was empty, and he only met a sleepy-eyed captain. It was not until two o'clock that they would begin to get up steam to resume work. First he went to take from a cupboard a jacket which he pretended to have forgotten. Various tools – a drill armed with its screw, a small but very strong saw, a hammer, and a chisel – were rolled up in this jacket. Then he left. But instead of going out through the shed he passed through the narrow corridor which led to the ladder passage. With his jacket under his arm he quietly went down without a lamp, measuring the depth by counting the ladders. He knew that the cage jarred at three hundred and seventy-four metres against the fifth row of the lower tubbing. When he had counted fifty-four ladders he put out his hand and was able to feel the swelling of the planking. It was there. Then, with the skill and coolness of a good workman who has been reflecting over his task for a long time, he set to work. He began by sawing a panel in the brattice so as to communicate with the winding-shaft. With the help of matches, quickly lighted and blown out, he was then able to ascertain the condition of the tubbing and of the recent repairs.

Between Calais and Valenciennes the sinking of mine shafts was surrounded by immense difficulties on account of the masses of subterranean water in great sheets at the level of the lowest valleys. Only the construction of tubbings, frameworks jointed like the stays of a barrel, could keep Out the springs which flow in and isolate the shafts in the midst of the lakes, which with deep obscure waves beat against the walls. It had been necessary in sinking the Voreux to establish two tubbings: that of the upper level, in the shifting sands and white clays bordering the chalky stratum, and fissured in every part, swollen with water like a sponge; then that of the lower level, immediately above the coal stratum, in a yellow sand as fine as flour, flowing with liquid fluidity; it was here that the Torrent was to be found, that subterranean sea so dreaded in the coal pits of the Nord, a sea with its storms and its shipwrecks, an unknown and unfathomable sea, rolling its dark floods more than three hundred metres beneath the daylight. Usually the tubbings resisted the enormous pressure; the only thing to be dreaded was the piling up of the neighbouring soil, shaken by the constant movement of the old galleries which were filling up. In this descent of the rocks lines of fracture were sometimes produced which slowly extended as far as the scaffolding, at last perforating it and pushing it into the shaft; and there was the great danger of a landslip and a flood filling the pit with an avalanche of earth and a deluge of springs.

Souvarine, sitting astride in the opening he had made, discovered a very serious defect in the fifth row of tubbing. The wood was bellied out from the framework; several planks had even come out of their shoulder-pieces. Abundant filtrations, *pichoux* the miners call them, were jetting out of the joints through the tarred oakum with which they were caulked. The carpenters, pressed for time, had been content to place iron squares at the angles, so carelessly that not all the screws were put in. A considerable movement was evidently going on behind in the sand of the Torrent.

Then with his wimble he unscrewed the squares so that another push would tear them all off. It was a foolhardy task, during which he frequently only just escaped from falling headlong down the hundred and eighty metres which separated him from the bottom. He had been obliged to seize the oak guides, the joists along which the cages slid; and suspended over the void he traversed the length of the cross-beams with which they were joined from point to point, slipping along, sitting down, turning over, simply buttressing himself on an elbow or a knee, with tranquil contempt of death. A breath would have sent him over, and three times he caught himself up without a shudder. First he felt with his hand and then worked, only lighting a match when he lost himself in the midst of these slimy beams. After loosening the screws he attacked the wood itself, and the peril became still greater. He had sought for the key, the piece which held the others; he attacked it furiously, making holes in it, sawing it, thinning it so that it lost its resistance; while through the holes and the cracks the water which escaped in small jets blinded him and soaked him in icy rain. Two matches were extinguished. They all be-came damp and then there was night, the bottomless depth of darkness.

From this moment he was seized by rage. The breath of the invisible intoxicated him, the black horror of this rain-beaten hole urged him to mad destruction. He wreaked his fury at random against the tubbing, striking where he could with his wimble, with his saw, seized by the desire to bring the whole thing at once down on his head. He brought as much ferocity to the task as though he had been digging a knife into the skin of some execrated living creature. He would kill the Voreux at last, that evil beast with ever-open jaws which had swallowed so much human flesh! The bite of his tools could be heard, his spine lengthened, he crawled, climbed down, then up again, holding on by a miracle, in continual movement, the flight of a nocturnal bird amid the scaffolding of a belfry.

But he grew calm, dissatisfied with himself. Why could not things be done coolly? Without haste he took breath, and then went back into the ladder passage, stopping up the hole by replacing the panel which he had sawn. That was enough; he did not wish to raise the alarm by excessive damage which would have been repaired immediately. The beast was wounded in the belly; we should see if it was still alive at night. And he had left his mark; the frightened world would know that the beast had not died a natural death. He took his time in methodically rolling up his tools in his jacket, and slowly climbed up the ladders. Then, when he had emerged from the pit without being seen, it did not even occur to him to go and change his clothes. Three o'clock struck. He remained standing on the road waiting.

At the same hour Étienne, who was not asleep, was disturbed by a slight sound in the thick night of the room. He distinguished the low breath of the children, and the snoring of Bonnemort and Maheude; while Jeanlin near him was breathing with a prolonged flute-like whistle. No doubt he had dreamed, and he was turning back when the noise began again. It was the creaking of a palliasse, the stifled effort of someone who is getting up. Then he imagined that Catherine must be ill.

"I say, is it you? What is the matter?" he asked in a low voice.

No one replied, and the snoring of the others continued. For five minutes nothing stirred. Then there was fresh creaking. Feeling certain this time that he was not mistaken, he crossed the room, putting his hands out into the darkness to feel the opposite bed. He was surprised to find the young girl sitting up, holding in her breath, awake and on the watch.

"Well! why don't you reply? What are you doing, then?"

At last she said:

"I'm getting up."

"Getting up at this hour?"

"Yes, I'm going back to work at the pit."

Étienne felt deeply moved, and sat down on the edge of the palliasse, while Catherine explained her reasons to him. She suffered too much by living thus in idleness, feeling continual looks of reproach weighing on her; she would rather run the risk of being knocked about down there by Chaval. And if her mother refused to take her money when she brought it, well! she was big enough to act for herself and make her own soup.

"Go away; I want to dress. And don't say anything, will you, if you want to be kind?"

But he remained near her; he had put his arms round her waist in a caress of grief and pity. Pressed one against the other in their shirts, they could feel the warmth of each other's naked flesh, at the edge of this bed, still moist with the night's sleep. She had at first tried to free herself; then she began to cry quietly, in her turn taking him by the neck to press him against her in a despairing clasp. And they remained, without any further desires, with the past of their unfortunate love, which they had not been able to satisfy. Was it, then, done with for ever? Would they never dare to love each other some day, now that they were free? It only needed a little happiness to dissipate their shame – that awkwardness which prevented them from coming together because of all sorts of ideas which they themselves could not read clearly.

"Go to bed again," she whispered. "I don't want to light up, it would wake mother. It is time; leave me."

He could not hear; he was pressing her wildly, with a heart drowned in immense sadness. The need for peace, an irresistible need for happiness, was carrying him away; and he saw himself married, in a neat little house, with no other ambition than to live and to die there, both of them together. He would be satisfied with bread; and if there were only enough for one, she should have it.

What was the good of anything else? Was there anything in life worth more?

But she was unfolding her naked arms.

"Please, leave me."

Then, in a sudden impulse, he said in her ear:

"Wait, I'm coming with you."

And he was himself surprised at what he had said. He had sworn never to go down again; whence then came this sudden decision, arising from his lips without thought of his, without even a moment's discussion? There was now such calm within him, so complete a cure of his doubts, that he persisted like a man saved by chance, who has at last found the only harbour from his torment. So he refused to listen to her when she became alarmed, understanding that he was devoting himself for her and fearing the ill words which would greet him at the pit. He laughed at everything; the placards promised pardon and that was enough.

"I want to work; that's my idea. Let us dress and make no noise."

They dressed themselves in the darkness, with a thousand precautions. She had secretly prepared her miner's clothes the evening before; he took a jacket and breeches from the cupboard; and they did not wash themselves for fear of knocking the bowl. All were asleep, but they had to cross the narrow passage where the mother slept. When they started, as ill luck would have it, they stumbled against a chair. She woke and asked drowsily:

"Eh! what is it?"

Catherine had stopped, trembling, and violently pressing Étienne's hand.

"It's me; don't trouble yourself," he said. "I feel stifled and am going outside to breathe a bit."

"Very well."

And Maheude fell asleep again. Catherine dared not stir. At last she went down into the parlour and divided a slice of bread-and-butter which she had reserved from a loaf given by a Montsou lady. Then they softly closed the door and went away.

Souvarine had remained standing near the Avantage, at the corner of the road. For half an hour he had been looking at the colliers who were returning to work in the darkness, passing by with the dull tramp of a herd. He was counting them, as a butcher counts his beasts at the entrance to the slaughter-house, and he was surprised at their number; even his pessimism had not foreseen that the number of cowards would have been so great. The stream continued to pass by, and he grew stiff, very cold, with clenched teeth and bright eyes.

But he started. Among the men passing by, whose faces he could not distinguish, he had just recognized one by his walk. He came forward and stopped him.

"Where are you going to?"

Étienne, in surprise, instead of replying, stammered:

"What! you've not set out yet!"

Then he confessed he was going back to the pit. No doubt he had sworn; only it could not be called life to wait with folded arms for things which would perhaps happen in a hundred years; and, besides, reasons of his own had decided him.

Souvarine had listened to him, shuddering. He seized him by the shoulder, and pushed him towards the settlement.

"Go home again; I want you to. Do you understand?" But Catherine having approached, he recognized her also. Étienne protested, declaring that he allowed no one to judge his conduct. And the engine-man's eyes went from the young girl to her companion, while he stepped back with a sudden, relinquishing movement. When there was a woman in a man's heart, that man was done for; he might die. Perhaps he saw again in a rapid vision his mistress hanging over there at Moscow that last link cut from his flesh, which had rendered him free of the lives of others and of his own life. He said simply:

"Go."

Étienne, feeling awkward, was delaying, and trying to find some friendly word, so as not to separate in this manner.

"Then you're still going?"

"Yes."

"Well, give me your hand, old chap. A pleasant journey, and no ill feeling."

The other stretched out an icy hand. Neither friend nor wife.

"Good-bye for good this time."

"Yes, good-bye."

And Souvarine, standing motionless in the darkness, watched Étienne and Catherine entering the Voreux.

Chapter 3

AT four o'clock the descent began. Dansaert, who was personally installed at the marker's office in the lamp cabin, wrote down the name of each worker who presented himself and had a lamp given to him. He took them all, without remark, keeping to the promise of the placards. When, however, he noticed Étienne and Catherine at the wicket, he started and became very red, and was opening his mouth to refuse their names; then, he contented himself with the triumph, and a jeer. Ah! ah! so the strong man was thrown? The Company was, then, in luck since the terrible Montsou wrestler had come back to it to ask for bread? Étienne silently took his lamp and went towards the shaft with the putter.

But it was there, in the receiving-room, that Catherine feared the mates' bad words. At the very entrance she recognized Chaval, in the midst of some twenty miners, waiting till a cage was free. He came furiously towards her, but the sight of Étienne stopped him. Then he affected to sneer with an offensive shrug of the shoulders.

Very good! he didn't care a hang, since the other had come to occupy the place that was still warm; good riddance! It only concerned the gentleman if he liked the leavings; and beneath the exhibition of this contempt he was again seized by a tremor of jealousy, and his eyes flamed. For the rest, the mates did not stir, standing silent, with eyes lowered. They contented themselves with casting a sidelong look at the new-comers; then, dejected and without anger, they again stared fixedly at the mouth of the shaft, with their lamps in their hands, shivering beneath their thin jackets, in the constant draughts of this large room. At last the cage was wedged on to the keeps, and they were ordered to get in. Catherine and Étienne were squeezed in one tram, already containing Pierron and two pikemen. Beside them, in the other tram, Chaval was loudly saying to Father Mouque that the directors had made a mistake in not taking advantage of the opportunity to free the pits of the blackguards who were corrupting them; but the old groom, who had already fallen back into the dog-like resignation of his existence, no longer grew angry over the death of his children, and simply replied by a gesture of conciliation.

The cage freed itself and slipped down into the darkness. No one spoke. Suddenly, when they were in the middle third of the descent, there was a terrible jarring. The iron creaked, and the men were thrown on to each other.

"By God!" growled Étienne, "are they going to flatten us? We shall end by being left here for good, with their confounded tubbing. And they talk about having repaired it!"

The cage had, however, cleared the obstacle. It was now descending beneath so violent a rain, like a storm, that the workmen anxiously listened to the pouring. A number of leaks must then have appeared in the caulking of the joints.

Pierron, who had been working for several days, when asked about it did not like to show his fear, which might be considered as an attack on the management, so he only replied:

"Oh, no danger! it's always like that. No doubt they've not had time to caulk the leaks."

The torrent was roaring over their heads, and they at last reached the pit-eye beneath a veritable waterspout. Not one of the captains had thought of climbing up the ladders to investigate the matter. The pump would be enough, the carpenters would examine the joints the following night. The reorganization of work in the galleries gave considerable trouble. Before allowing the pikemen to return to their hewing cells, the engineer had decided that for the first five days all the men should execute certain works of consolidation which were extremely urgent. Landslips were threatening everywhere; the passages had suffered to such an extent that the timbering had to be repaired along a length of several hundred metres. Gangs of ten men were therefore formed below, each beneath the control of a captain. Then they were set to work at the most damaged spots. When the descent was complete, it was found that three hundred and twenty-two miners had gone down, about half of those who worked there when the pit was in full swing.

Chaval belonged to the same gang as Catherine and Étienne. This was not by chance; he had at first hidden behind his mates, and had then forced the captain s hand. This gang went to the end of the north gallery, nearly three kilometres away, to clear out a landslip which was stopping up a gallery in the Dix-Huit-Pouces seam. They attacked the fallen rocks with shovel and pick. Étienne, Chaval, and five others cleared away the rubbish while Catherine, with two trammers, wheeled the earth up to the upbrow. They seldom spoke, and the captain never left them. The putter's two lovers, however, were on the point of coming to blows. While growling that he had had enough of this trollop, Chaval was still thinking of her, and slyly hustling her about, so that Étienne had threatened to settle him if he did not leave her alone. They eyed each other fiercely, and had to be separated.

Towards eight o'clock Dansaert passed to give a glance at the work. He appeared to be in a very bad humour, and was furious with the captain; nothing had gone well, what was the meaning of such work, the planking would everywhere have to be done over again! And he went away declaring that he would come back with the engineer. He had been waiting for Négrel since morning, and could not understand the cause of this delay.

Another hour passed by. The captain had stopped the removal of the rubbish to employ all his people in supporting the roof. Even the putter and the two trammers left off wheeling to prepare and bring pieces of timber. At this end of the gallery the gang formed a sort of advance guard at the very extremity of the mine, now without communication with the other stalls. Three or four times strange noises, distant rushes, made the workers turn their heads to listen. What was it, then? One would have said that the passages were being emptied and the mates already returning at a running pace. But the sound was lost in the deep silence, and they set to wedging their wood again, dazed by the loud blows of the hammer. At last they returned to the rubbish, and the wheeling began once more. Catherine came back from her first journey in terror, saying that no one was to be found at the upbrow.

"I called, but there was no reply. They've all cleared out of the place."

The bewilderment was so great that the ten men threw down their tools to rush away. The idea that they were abandoned, left alone at the bottom of the mine, so far from the pit-eye, drove them wild. They only kept their lamp and ran in single file – the men, the boys, the putter; the captain himself lost his head and shouted out appeals, more and more frightened at the silence in this endless desert of galleries. What then had happened that they did not meet a soul? What accident could thus have driven away their mates? Their terror was increased by the uncertainty of the danger, this threat which they felt there without knowing what it was.

When they at last came near the pit-eye, a torrent barred their road. They were at once in water to the knees, and were no longer able to run, laboriously fording the flood with the thought that one minute's delay might mean death.

"By God! it's the tubbing that's given way," cried Étienne. "I said we should be left here for good."

Since the descent Pierron had anxiously observed the increase of the deluge which fell from the shaft. As with two others he loaded the trains he raised his head, his face covered with large drops, and his ears ringing with the roar of the tempest above. But he trembled especially when he noticed that the sump beneath him, that pit ten metres deep. was filling; the water was already spurting through the floor and covering the metal plates. This showed that the pump was no longer sufficient to fight against the leaks. He heard it panting with the groan of fatigue. Then he warned Dansaert, who swore angrily,. replying that they must wait for the engineer. Twice he returned to the charge without extracting anything else but exasperated shrugs of the shoulder. Well! the water was rising; what could he do?

Mouque appeared with Bataille, whom he was leading to work, and he had to hold him with both hands, for the sleepy old horse had suddenly reared up, and, with a shrill neigh, was stretching his head towards the shaft. "Well, philosopher, what troubles you? Ah! it's because it rains. Come along, that doesn't concern you."

But the beast quivered all over his skin, and Mouque forcibly drew him to the haulage gallery.

Almost at the same moment as Mouque and Bataille were disappearing at the end of a gallery, there was a crackling in the air, followed by the prolonged noise of a fall. It was a piece of tubbing which had got loose and was falling a hundred and eighty metres down, rebounding against the walls. Pierron and the other porters were able to get out of the way, and the oak plank only smashed an empty tram. At the same time, a mass of water, the leaping flood of a broken dyke, rushed down. Dansaert proposed to go up and examine; but, while he was still speaking, another piece rolled down. And in terror before the threatening catastrophe, he no longer hesitated, but gave the order to go up, sending captains to warn the men in their stalls.

Then a terrible hustling began. From every gallery rows of workers came rushing up, trying to take the cages by assault. They crushed madly against each other in order to be taken up at once. Some who had thought of trying the ladder passage came down again shouting that it was already stopped up. That was the terror they all felt each time that the cage rose; this time it was able to pass, but who knew if it would be able to pass again in the midst of the obstacles obstructing the shaft? The downfall must be continuing above, for a series of low detonations was heard, the planks were splitting and bursting amid the continuous and increasing roar of a storm. One cage soon became useless, broken in and no longer sliding between the guides, which were doubtless broken. The other jarred to such a degree that the cable would certainly break soon. And there remained a hundred men to be taken up, all panting, clinging to one another, bleeding and half-drowned. Two were killed by falls of planking. A third, who had seized the cage, fell back fifty metres up and disappeared in the sump.

Dansaert, however, was trying to arrange matters in an orderly manner. Armed with a pick he threatened to open the skull of the first man who refused to obey; and he tried to arrange them in file, shouting that the porters were to go up last after having sent up their mates. He was not listened to, and he had to prevent the pale and cowardly Pierron from entering among the first. At each departure he pushed him aside with a blow. But his own teeth were chattering, a minute more and he would be swallowed up; everything was smashing up there, a flood had broken loose, a murderous rain of scaffolding. A few men were still running up when, mad with fear, he jumped into a tram, allowing Pierron to jump in behind him. The cage rose.

At this moment the gang to which Étienne and Chaval belonged had just reached the pit-eye. They saw the cage disappear and rushed forward, but they had to draw back from the final downfall of the tubbing; the shaft was stopped up and the cage would not come down again. Catherine was sobbing, and Chaval was choked with shouting oaths. There were twenty of them; were those bloody bosses going to abandon them thus? Father Mouque, who had brought back Bataille without hurrying, was still holding him by the bridle, both of them stupefied, the man and the beast, in the face of this rapid flow of the inundation. The water was already rising to their thighs. Étienne in silence, with clenched teeth, supported Catherine between his arms. And the twenty yelled with their faces turned up, obstinately gazing at the shaft like imbeciles, that shifting hole which was belching out a flood and from which no help could henceforth come to them.

At the surface, Dansaert, on arriving, perceived Négrel running up. By some fatality, Madame Hennebeau had that morning delayed him on rising, turning over the leaves of catalogues for the purchase of wedding presents. It was ten o'clock.

"Well! what's happening, then?" he shouted from afar.

"The pit is ruined," replied the head captain.

And he described the catastrophe in a few stammered words, while the engineer incredulously shrugged his shoulders. What! could tubbing be demolished like that? They were exaggerating; he would make an examination.

"I suppose no one has been left at the bottom?"

Dansaert was confused. No, no one; at least, so he hoped. But some of the men might have been delayed.

"But," said Négrel, "what in the name of creation have you come up for, then? You can't leave your men!"

He immediately gave orders to count the lamps. In the morning three hundred and twenty-two had been distributed, and now only two hundred and fifty-five could be found; but several men acknowledged that in the hustling and panic they had dropped theirs and left them behind. An attempt was made to call over the men, but it was impossible to establish the exact number. Some of the miners had gone away, others did not hear their names. No one was agreed as to the number of the missing mates. It might be twenty, perhaps forty. And the engineer could only make out one thing with certainty: there were men down below, for their yells could be distinguished through the sound of the water and the fallen scaffolding, on leaning over the mouth of the shaft.

Négrel's first care was to send for M. Hennebeau, and to try to close the pit; but it was already too late. The colliers who had rushed to the Deux-Cent-Quarante settlement, as though pursued by the cracking tubbing, had frightened the families; and bands of women, old men, and little ones came running up, shaken by cries and sobs. They had to be pushed back, and a line of overseers was formed to keep them off, for they would have interfered with the operations. Many of the men who had come up from the shaft remained there stupidly without thinking of changing their clothes, riveted by fear before this terrible hole in which they had nearly remained for ever. The women, rushing wildly around them, implored them for names. Was So-and-so among them? and that one? and this one? They did not know, they stammered; they shuddered terribly, and made gestures like madmen, gestures which seemed to be pushing away some abominable vision which was always present to them. The crowd rapidly increased, and lamentations arose from the roads. And up there on the pit-bank, in Bonnemort's cabin, on the ground was seated a man, Souvarine, who had not gone away, who was looking on.

"The names! the names!" cried the women, with voices choked by tears.

Négrel appeared for a moment, and said hurriedly:

"As soon as we know the names they shall be given out, but nothing is lost so far: every one will be saved. I am going down."

Then, silent with anguish, the crowd waited. The engineer, in fact, with quiet courage was preparing to go down. He had had the cage unfastened, giving orders to replace it at the end of the cable by a tub; and as he feared that the water would extinguish his lamp, he had another fastened beneath the tub, which would protect it.

Several captains, trembling and with white, disturbed faces, assisted in these preparations.

"You will come with me, Dansaert," said Négrel, abruptly.

Then, when he saw them all without courage, and that the head captain was tottering, giddy with terror, he pushed him aside with a movement of contempt.

"No, you will be in my way. I would rather go alone." He was already in the narrow bucket, which swayed at the end of the cable; and holding his lamp in one hand and the signal-cord in the other, he shouted to the engine-man:

"Gently!"

The engine set the drums in movement, and Négrel disappeared in the gulf, from which the yells of the wretches below still arose.

At the upper part nothing had moved. He found that the tubbing here was in good condition. Balanced in the middle of the shaft he lighted up the walls as he turned round; the leaks between the joints were so slight that his lamp did not suffer. But at three hundred metres, when he reached the lower tubbing, the lamp was extinguished, as he expected, for a jet had filled the tub. After that he was only able to see by the hanging lamp which preceded him in the darkness, and, in spite of his courage, he shuddered and turned pale in the face of the horror of the disaster. A few pieces of timber alone remained; the others had fallen in with their frames. Behind, enormous cavities had been hollowed out, and the yellow sand, as fine as flour, was flowing in considerable masses; while the waters of the Torrent, that subterranean sea with its unknown tempests and shipwrecks, were discharging in a flow like a weir. He went down lower, lost in the midst of these chasms which continued to multiply, beaten and turned round by the waterspout of the springs, so badly lighted by the red star of the lamp moving on below, that he seemed to distinguish the roads and squares of some destroyed town far away in the play of the great moving shadows. No human work was any longer possible. His only remaining hope was to attempt to save the men in peril. As he sank down he heard the cries becoming louder, and he was obliged to stop; an impassable obstacle barred the shaft – a mass of scaffolding, the broken joists of the guides, the split brattices entangled with the metal-work torn from the pump. As he looked on for a long time with aching heart, the yelling suddenly ceased. No doubt, the rapid rise of the water had forced the wretches to flee into the galleries, if, indeed, the flood had not already filled their mouths.

Négrel resigned himself to pulling the signal-cord as a sign to draw up. Then he had himself stopped again. He could not conceive the cause of this sudden accident. He wished to investigate it, and examined those pieces of the tubbing which were still in place. At a distance the tears and cuts in the wood had surprised him. His lamp, drowned in dampness, was going out, and, touching with his fingers, he clearly recognized the marks of the saw and of the wimble – the whole abominable labour of destruction. Evidently this catastrophe had been intentionally produced. He was stupefied, and the pieces of timber, cracking and falling down with their frames in a last slide, nearly carried him with them. His courage fled. The thought of the man who had done that made his hair stand on end, and froze him with a supernatural fear of evil, as though, mixed with the darkness, the man were still there paying for his immeasurable crime. He shouted and shook the cord furiously; and it was, indeed, time, for he perceived that the uppertubbing, a hundred metres higher, was in its turn beginning to move. The joints were opening, losing their oakum caulking, and streams were rushing through. It was now only a question of hours before the tubbing would all fall down.

At the surface M. Hennebeau was anxiously waiting for Négrel.

"Well, what?" he asked.

But the engineer was choked, and could not speak; he felt faint.

"It is not possible; such a thing was never seen. Have you examined?"

He nodded with a cautious look. He refused to talk in the presence of some captains who were listening, and led his uncle ten metres away, and not thinking this far enough, drew still farther back; then, in a low whisper, he at last told of the outrage, the torn and sawn planks, the pit bleeding at the neck and groaning. Turning pale, the manager also lowered his voice, with that instinctive need of silence in face of the monstrosity of great orgies and great crimes. It was useless to look as though they were trembling before the ten thousand Montsou men; later on they would see. And they both continued whispering, overcome at the thought that a man had had the courage to go down, to hang in the midst of space, to risk his life twenty times over in his terrible task. They could not even understand this mad courage in destruction; they refused to believe, in spite of the evidence, just as we doubt those stories of celebrated escapes of prisoners who fly through windows thirty metres above the ground.

When M. Hennebeau came back to the captains a nervous spasm was drawing his face. He made a gesture of despair, and gave orders that the mine should be evacuated at once. It was a kind of funeral procession, in silent abandonment, with glances thrown back at those great masses of bricks, empty and still standing, but which nothing henceforth could save.

And as the manager and the engineer came down last from the receiving-room, the crowd met them with its clamour, repeating obstinately:

"The names! the names! Tell us the names!"

Maheude was now there, among the women. She recollected the noise in the night; her daughter and the lodger must have gone away together, and they were certainly down at the bottom. And after having cried that it was a good thing, that they deserved to stay there, the heartless cowards, she had run up, and was standing in the first row, trembling with anguish. Besides, she no longer dared to doubt; the discussion going on around her informed her as to the names of those who were down. Yes, yes, Catherine was among them, Étienne also – a mate had seen them. But there was not always agreement with regard to the others. No, not this one; on the contrary, that one, perhaps Chaval, with whom, however, a trammer declared that he had ascended. The Levaque and Pierronne, although none of their people were in danger, cried out and lamented as loudly as the others. Zacharie, who had come up among the first, in spite of his inclination to make fun of everything had weepingly kissed his wife and mother, and remained near the latter, quivering, and showing an unexpected degree of affection for his sister, refusing to believe that she was below so long as the bosses made no authoritative statement.

"The names! the names! For pity's sake, the names!"

Négrel, who was exhausted, shouted to the overseers:

"Can't you make them be still? It's enough to kill one with vexation! We don't know the names!"

Two hours passed away in this manner. In the first terror no one had thought of the other shaft at the old Réquillart mine, M. Hennebeau was about to announce that the rescue would be attempted from that side, when a rumour ran round: five men had just escaped the inundation by climbing up the rotten ladders of the old unused passage, and Father Mouque was named. This caused surprise, for no one knew he was below. But the narrative of the five who had escaped increased the weeping; fifteen mates had not been able to follow them, having gone astray, and been walled up by falls. And it was no longer possible to assist them, for there were already ten metres of water in Réquillart. All the names were known, and the air was filled with the groans of a slaughtered multitude.

"Will you make them be still?" Négrel repeated furiously. "Make them draw back! Yes, yes, to a hundred metres! There is danger; push them back, push them back!"

It was necessary to struggle against these poor people. They were imagining all sorts of misfortunes, and they had to be driven away so that the deaths might be concealed; the captains explained to them that the shaft would destroy the whole mine. This idea rendered them mute with terror, and they at last allowed themselves to be driven back step by step; the guards, however, who kept them back had to be doubled, for they were fascinated by the spot and continually returned. Thousands of people were hustling each other along the road; they were running up from all the settlements, and even from Montsou. And the man above, on the pit-bank, the fair man with the girlish face, smoked

cigarettes to occupy himself, keeping
his clear eyes fixed on the pit.

Then the wait began. It was midday; no
one had eaten, but no one moved away.
In the misty sky, of a dirty grey colour,
rusty clouds were slowly passing by. A
big dog, behind Rasseneur's hedge, was
barking furiously without cessation,
irritated by the living breath of the
crowd. And the crowd had gradually
spread over the neighbouring ground,
forming a circle at a hundred metres
round the pit. The Voreux arose in the
centre of the great space. There was not
a soul there, not a sound; it was a
desert. The windows and the doors, left
open, showed the abandonment within;
a forgotten ginger cat, divining the peril
in this solitude, jumped from a staircase
and disappeared. No doubt the stoves
of the boilers were scarcely extinguished, for the tall brick chimney gave
out a light smoke beneath the dark
clouds; while the weathercock on the
steeple creaked in the wind with a short,
shrill cry, the only melancholy voice of

these vast buildings which were about to die.

At two o'clock nothing had moved, M. Hennebeau, Négrel, and other engineers who had hastened up, formed a group in black coats and hats standing in front of the crowd; and they, too, did not move away, though their legs were aching with fatigue, and they were feverish and ill at their impotence in the face of such a disaster, only whispering occasional words as though at a dying person's bedside. The upper tubbing must nearly all have fallen in, for sudden echoing sounds could be heard as of deep broken falls, succeeded by silence. The wound was constantly enlarging; the landslip which had begun below was rising and approaching the surface. Négrel was seized by nervous impatience; he wanted to see, and he was already advancing alone into this awful void when he was seized by the shoulders. What was the good? he could prevent nothing. An old miner, however, circumventing the overseers, rushed into the shed; but he quietly reappeared, he had gone for his sabots.

Three o'clock struck. Still nothing. A falling shower had soaked the crowd, but they had not withdrawn a step. Rasseneur's dog had begun to bark again. And it was at twenty minutes past three only that the first shock was felt. The Voreux trembled, but continued solid and upright. Then a second shock followed immediately, and a long cry came from open mouths; the tarred screening-shed, after having tottered twice, had fallen down with a terrible crash. Beneath the enormous pressure the structures broke and jarred each other so powerfully that sparks leapt out. From this moment the earth continued to tremble, the shocks succeeded one another, subterranean downfalls, the rumbling of a volcano in eruption. Afar the dog was no longer barking, but he howled plaintively as though announcing the oscillations which he felt coming; and the women, the children, all these people who were looking on, could not keep back a clamour of distress at each of these blows which shook them. In less than ten minutes the slate roof of the steeple fell in, the receiving-room and the engine-rooms were split open, leaving a considerable breach. Then the sounds ceased, the downfall stopped, and there was again deep silence.

For an hour the Voreux remained thus, broken into, as though bombarded by an army of barbarians. There was no more crying out; the enlarged circle of spectators merely looked on. Beneath the piled-up beams of the sifting-shed, fractured tipping cradles could be made out with broken and twisted hoppers. But the rubbish had especially accumulated at the receiving-room, where there had been a rain of bricks, and large portions of wall and masses of plaster had fallen in. The iron scaffold which bore the pulleys had bent, half-buried in the pit; a cage was still suspended, a torn cable-end was hanging; then there was a hash of trains, metal plates, and ladders. By some chance the lamp cabin remained standing, exhibiting on the left its bright rows of little lamps. And at the end of its disembowelled chamber, the engine could be seen seated squarely on its massive foundation of masonry; its copper was shining and its huge steel limbs seemed to possess indestructible muscles. The enormous crank, bent in the air, looked like the powerful knee of some giant quietly reposing in his strength.

After this hour of respite, M. Hennebeau's hopes began to rise. The movement of the soil must have come to an end, and there would be some chance of saving the engine and the remainder of the buildings. But he would not yet allow any one to approach, considering another half-hour's patience desirable. This waiting became unbearable; the hope increased the anguish and all hearts were beating quickly. A dark cloud, growing large at the horizon, hastened the twilight, a sinister nightfall over this wreck of earth's tempests. Since seven o'clock they had been there without moving or eating.

And suddenly, as the engineers were cautiously advancing, a supreme convulsion of the soil put them to flight.

Subterranean detonations broke out; a whole monstrous artillery was cannonading in the gulf. At the surface, the last buildings were tipped over and crushed. At first a sort of whirlpool carried away the rubbish from the sifting-shed and the receiving-room. Next, the boiler building burst and disappeared. Then it was the low square tower, where the pumping-engine was groaning, which fell on its face like a man mown down by a bullet. And then a terrible thing was seen; the engine, dislocated from its massive foundation, with broken limbs was struggling against death; it moved, it straightened its crank, its giant's knee, as though to rise; but, crushed and swallowed up, it was dying. The chimney alone, thirty metres high, still remained standing, though shaken, like a mast in the tempest. It was thought that it would be crushed to fragments and fly to powder, when suddenly it sank in one block, drunk down by the earth, melted like a colossal candle; and nothing was left, not even the point of the lightning conductor. It was done for; the evil beast crouching in this hole, gorged with human flesh, was no longer breathing with its thick, long respiration. The Voreux had been swallowed whole by the abyss.

The crowd rushed away yelling. The women hid their eyes as they ran. Terror drove the men along like a pile of dry leaves. They wished not to shout and they shouted, with swollen breasts, and arms in the air, before the immense hole which had been hollowed out. This crater, as of an extinct volcano, fifteen metres deep, extended from the road to the canal for a space of at least forty metres. The whole square of the mine had followed the buildings, the gigantic platforms, the footbridges with their rails, a complete train of trams, three wagons; without counting the wood supply, a forest of cut timber, gulped down like straw. At the bottom it was only possible to distinguish a confused mass of beams, bricks, iron, plaster, frightful remains, piled up, entangled, soiled in the fury of the catastrophe. And the hole became larger, cracks started from the edges, reaching afar, across the fields. A fissure ascended as far as Rasseneur's bar, and his front wall had cracked. Would the settlement itself pass into it? How far ought they to flee to reach shelter at the end of this abominable day, beneath this leaden cloud which also seemed about to crush the earth?

A cry of pain escaped Négrel. M. Hennebeau, who had drawn back, was in tears. The disaster was not complete; one bank of the canal gave way, and the canal emptied itself like one bubbling sheet through one of the cracks. It disappeared there, falling like a cataract down a deep valley. The mine drank down this river; the galleries would now be submerged for years. Soon the crater was filled and a lake of muddy water occupied the place where once stood the Voreux, like one of those lakes beneath which sleep accursed towns. There was a terrified silence, and nothing now could be heard but the fall of this water rumbling in the bowels of the earth.

Then on the shaken pit-bank Souvarine rose up. He had recognized Maheude and Zacharie sobbing before this downfall, the weight of which was so heavy on the heads of the wretches who were in agony beneath. And he threw down his last cigarette; he went away, without looking back, into the now dark night. Afar his shadow diminished and mingled with the darkness. He was going over there, to the unknown. He was going tranquilly to extermination, wherever there might be dynamite to blow up towns and men. He will be there, without doubt, when the middle class in agony shall hear the pavement of the streets bursting up beneath their feet.

Chapter 4

ON the night that followed the collapse of the Voreux M. Hennebeau started for Paris, wishing to inform the directors in person before the newspapers published the news. And when he returned on the following day he appeared to be quite calm, with his usual correct administrative air. He had evidently freed himself from responsibility; he did not appear to have decreased in favour. On the contrary, the decree appointing him officer of the Legion of Honour was signed twenty-four hours afterwards.

But if the manager remained safe, the Company was tottering beneath the terrible blow. It was not the few million francs that had been lost, it was the wound in the flank, the deep incessant fear of the morrow in face of this massacre of one of their mines. The Company was so impressed that once more it felt the need of silence. What was the good of stirring up this abomination? If the villain were discovered, why make a martyr of him in order that his awful heroism might turn other heads, and give birth to a long line of incendiaries and murderers? Besides, the real culprit was not suspected. The Company came to think that there was an army of accomplices, not being able to believe that a single man could have had courage and strength for such a task; and it was precisely this thought which weighed on them, this thought of an ever-increasing threat to the existence of their mines. The manager had received orders to organize a vast system of espionage, and then to dismiss quietly, one by one, the dangerous men who were suspected of having had a hand in the crime. They contented themselves with this method of purification – a prudent and politic method.

There was only one immediate dismissal, that of Dansaert, the head captain. Ever since the scandal at Pierronne's house he had become impossible. A pretext was made of his attitude in danger, the cowardice of a captain abandoning his men. This was also a prudent sop thrown to the miners, who hated him.

Among the public, however, many rumours had circulated, and the directors had to send a letter of correction to one newspaper, contradicting a story in which mention was made of a barrel of powder lighted by the strikers. After a rapid inquiry the Government inspector had concluded that there had been a natural rupture of the tubbing, occasioned by the piling up of the soil; and the Company had preferred to be silent, and to accept the blame of a lack of superintendence. In the Paris press, after the third day, the catastrophe had served to increase the stock of general news; nothing was talked of but the men perishing at the bottom of the mine, and the telegrams published every morning were eagerly read. At Montsou people grew pale and speechless at the very name of the Voreux, and a legend had formed which made the boldest tremble as they whispered it. The whole country showed great pity for the victims; visits were organized to the destroyed pit, and whole families hastened up to shudder at the ruins which lay so heavily over the heads of the buried wretches.

Deneulin, who had been appointed divisional engineer, came into the midst of the disaster on beginning his duties; and his first care was to turn the canal back into its bed, for this torrent increased the damage every hour. Extensive works were necessary, and he at once set a hundred men to construct a dyke. Twice over the impetuosity of the stream carried away the first dams. Now pumps were set up and a furious struggle was going on; step by step the vanished soil was being violently reconquered.

But the rescue of the engulfed miners was a still more absorbing work. Négrel was appointed to attempt a supreme effort, and arms were not lacking to help him; all the colliers rushed to offer themselves in an outburst of brotherhood. They forgot the strike, they did not trouble themselves at all about payment; they might get nothing, they only asked to risk their lives as soon as there were mates in danger of death. They were all there with their tools, quivering as they waited to know where they ought to strike. Many of them, sick with fright after the accident, shaken by nervous tremors, soaked in cold sweats, and the prey of continual nightmares, got up in spite of everything, and were as eager as any in their desire to fight against the earth, as though they had a revenge to take on it. Unfortunately, the difficulty began when the question arose, What could be done? how could they go down? from what side could they attack the rocks?

Négrel's opinion was that not one of the unfortunate people was alive; the fifteen had surely perished, drowned or suffocated. But in these mine catastrophes the rule is always to assume that buried men are alive, and he acted on this supposition. The first problem which he proposed to himself was to decide where they could have taken refuge. The captains and old miners whom he consulted were agreed on one point: in the face of the rising water the men had certainly come up from gallery to gallery to the highest cuttings, so that they were, without doubt, driven to the end of some upper passages. This agreed with Father Mouque's information, and his confused narrative even gave reason to suppose that in the wild flight the band had separated into smaller groups, leaving fugitives on the road at every level. But the captains were not unanimous when the discussion of possible attempts at rescue arose. As the passages nearest to the surface were a hundred and fifty metres down, there could be no question of sinking a shaft. Réquillart remained the one means of access, the only point by which they could approach. The worst was that the old pit, now also inundated, no longer communicated with the Voreux; and above the level of the water only a few ends of galleries belonging to the first level were left free. The pumping process would require years, and the best plan would be to visit these galleries and ascertain if any of them approached the submerged passages at the end of which the distressed miners were suspected to be. Before logically arriving at this point, much discussion had been necessary to dispose of a crowd of impracticable plans.

Négrel now began to stir up the dust of the archives; he discovered the old plans of the two pits, studied them, and decided on the points at which their investigations ought to be carried on. Gradually this hunt excited him; he was, in his turn, seized by a fever of devotion, in spite of his ironical indifference to men and things. The first difficulty was in going down at Réquillart; it was necessary to clear out the rubbish from the mouth of the shaft, to cut down the mountain ash, and raze the sloes and the hawthorns; they had also repair the ladders. Then they began to feel around. The engineer, having gone down with ten workmen, made them strike the iron of their tools against certain parts of the seam which he pointed out to them; and in deep silence they each placed an ear to the coal, listening for any distant blows to reply. But they went in vain through every practicable gallery; no echo returned to them. Their embarrassment increased. At what spot should they cut into the bed?

Towards whom should they go, since no once appeared to be there? They persisted in seeking, however, notwithstanding the exhaustion produced by their growing anxiety.

From the first day, Maheude came in the morning to Réquillart. She sat down on a beam in front of the shaft, and did not stir from it till evening. When a man came up, she rose and questioned him with her eyes:

Nothing? No, nothing! And she sat down again, and waited still, without a word, with hard, fixed face. Jeanlin also, seeing that his den was invaded, prowled around with the frightened air of a beast of prey whose burrow will betray his booty. He thought of the little soldier lying beneath the rocks, fearing lest they should trouble his sound sleep; but that side of the mine was beneath the water, and, besides, their investigations were directed more to the left, in the west gallery. At first, Philoméne had also come, accompanying Zacharie, who was one of the gang; then she became wearied at catching cold, without need or result, and went back to the settlement, dragging through her days, a limp, indifferent woman, occupied from morning to night in coughing. Zacharie on the contrary, lived for nothing else; he would have devoured the soil to get back his sister. At night he shouted out that he saw, her, he heard her, very lean from hunger, her chest sore with calling for help. Twice he had tried to dig without orders, saying that it was there, that he was sure of it. The engineer would not let him go down any more, and he would not go away from the pit, from which he was driven off; he could not even sit down and wait near his mother, he was so deeply stirred by the need to act, which drove him constantly on.

It was the third day. Négrel, in despair, had resolved to abandon the attempt in the evening. At midday, after lunch, when he came back with his men to make one last effort, he was surprised to see Zacharie, red and gesticulating, come out of the mine shouting:

"She's there! She's replied to me! Come along, quickly!"

He had slid down the ladders, in spite of the watchman, and was declaring that he had heard hammering over there, in the first passage of the Guillaume seam.

"But we have already been twice in that direction," Négrel observed, sceptically. "Anyhow, we'll go and see."

Maheude had risen, and had to be prevented from going down. She waited, standing at the edge of the shaft, gazing down into the darkness of the hole.

Négrel, down below, himself struck three blows, at long intervals. He then applied his ear to the coal, cautioning the workers to be very silent. Not a sound reached him, and he shook his head; evidently the poor lad was dreaming. In a fury, Zacharie struck in his turn, and listened anew with bright eyes, and limbs trembling with joy. Then the other workmen tried the experiment, one after the other, and all grew animated, hearing the distant reply quite clearly. The engineer was astonished; he again applied his ear, and was at last able to catch a sound of aerial softness, a rhythmical roll scarcely to be distinguished, the well-known cadence beaten by the miners when they are fighting against the coal in the midst of danger. The coal transmits the sound with crystalline limpidity for a very great distance. A captain who was there estimated that the thickness of the block which separated them from their mates could not be less than fifty metres. But it seemed as if they could already stretch out a hand to them, and general gladness broke out. Négrel decided to begin at once the work of approach.

When Zacharie, up above, saw Maheude again, they embraced each other.

"It won't do to get excited," Pierronne, who had come for a visit of inquisitiveness, was cruel enough to say. "If Catherine isn't there, it would be such a grief afterwards!"

That was true; Catherine might be somewhere else. "Just leave me alone, will you? Damn it!" cried Zacharie in a rage. "She's there; I know it!"

Maheude sat down again in silence, with motionless face, continuing to wait.

As soon as the story was spread at Montsou, a new crowd arrived. Nothing was to be seen; but they remained there all the same, and had to be kept at a distance. Down below, the work went on day and night. For fear of meeting an obstacle, the engineer had had three descending galleries opened in the seam, converging to the point where the enclosed miners were supposed to be. Only one pikeman could hew at the coal on the narrow face of the tube; he was relieved every two hours, and the coal piled in baskets was passed up, from hand to hand, by a chain of men, increased as the hole was hollowed out. The work at first proceeded very quickly; they did six metres a day.

Zacharie had secured a place among the workers chosen for the hewing. It was a post of honour which was disputed over, and he became furious when they wished to relieve him after his regulation two hours of labour. He robbed his mates of their turn, and refused to let go the pick. His gallery was soon in advance of the others. He fought against the coal so fiercely that his breath could be heard coming from the tube like the roar of a forge within his breast. When he came out, black and muddy, dizzy with fatigue, he fell to the ground and had to be wrapped up in a covering. Then, still tottering, he plunged back again, and the struggle began anew – the low, deep blows, the stifled groans, the victorious fury of massacre. The worst was that the coal now became hard; he twice broke his tool, and was exasperated that he could not get on so fast. He suffered also from the heat, which increased with every metre of advance, and was unbearable at the end of this narrow hole where the air could not circulate. A hand ventilator worked well, but aeration was so inadequate that on three occasions it was necessary to take out fainting hewers who were being asphyxiated.

Négrel lived below with his men. His meals were sent down to him, and he sometimes slept for a couple of hours on a truss of straw, rolled in a cloak. The one thing that kept them up was the supplication of the wretches beyond, the call which was sounded ever more distinctly to hasten on the rescue. It now rang very clearly with a musical sonority, as though struck on the plates of a harmonica. It led them on; they advanced to this crystalline sound as men advance to the sound of cannon in battle. Every time that a pikeman was relieved, Négrel went down and struck, then applied his ear; and every time, so far, the reply had come, rapid and urgent. He had no doubt remaining; they were advancing in the right direction, but with what fatal slowness! They would never arrive soon enough. On the first two days they had indeed hewn through thirteen metres; but on the third day they fell to five, and then on the fourth to three. The coal was becoming closer and harder, to such an extent that they now with difficulty struck through two metres. On the ninth day, after superhuman efforts, they had advanced thirty-two metres, and calculated that some twenty must still be left before them. For the prisoners it was the beginning of the twelfth day; twelve times over had they passed twenty-four hours without bread, without fire, in that icy darkness! This awful idea moistened the eyelids and stiffened the arm of the workers. It seemed impossible that Christians could live longer. The distant blows had become weaker since the previous day, and every moment they trembled lest they should stop.

Maheude came regularly every morning to sit at the mouth of the shaft. In her arms she brought Estelle, who could not remain alone from morning to night. Hour by hour she followed the workers, sharing their hopes and fears. There was feverish expectation among the groups standing around, and even as far as Montsou, with endless discussion. Every heart in the district was beating down there beneath the earth.

On the ninth day, at the breakfast hour, no reply came from Zacharie when he was called for the relay. He was like a madman, working on furiously with oaths. Négrel, who had come up for a moment, was not there to make him obey, and only a captain and three miners were below. No doubt Zacharie, infuriate with the feeble vacillating light, which delayed his work, committed the imprudence of opening his lamp, although severe orders had been given for leakages of fire-damp had taken place, and the gas remained in enormous masses in these narrow, unventilated passages. Suddenly, a roar of thunder was heard, and a spout of fire darted out of the tube as from the mouth of a cannon charged with grapeshot. Everything flamed up and the air caught fire like powder, from one end of the galleries to the other. This torrent of flame carried away the captain and three workers, ascended the pit, and leapt up to the daylight in an eruption which split the rocks and the ruins around. The inquisitive fled, and Maheude arose, pressing the frightened Estelle to her breast.

When Négrel and the men came back they were seized by a terrible rage. They struck their heels on the earth as on a stepmother who was killing her children at random in the imbecile whims of her cruelty. They were devoting themselves, they were coming to the help of their mates, and still they must lose some of their men! After three long hours of effort and danger they reached the galleries once more, and the melancholy ascent of the victims took place. Neither the captain nor the workers were dead, but they were covered by awful wounds which gave out an odour of grilled flesh; they had drunk of fire, the burns had got into their throats, and they constantly moaned and prayed to be finished off. One of the three miners was the man who had smashed the pump at Gaston-Marie with a final blow of the shovel during the strike; the two others still had scars on their hands, and grazed, torn fingers from the energy with which they had thrown bricks at the soldiers. The pale and shuddering crowd took off their hats when they were carried by.

Maheude stood waiting. Zacharie's body at last appeared. The clothes were burnt, the body was nothing but black charcoal, calcined and unrecognizable. The head had been smashed by the explosion and no longer existed. And when these awful remains were placed on a stretcher, Maheude followed them mechanically, her burning eyelids without a tear. With Estelle drowsily lying in her arms, she went along, a tragic figure, her hair lashed by the wind. At the settlement Philoméne seemed stupid; her eyes were turned into fountains and she was quickly relieved. But the mother had already returned with the same step to Réquillart; she had accompanied her son, she was returning to wait for her daughter.

Three more days passed by. The rescue work had been resumed amid incredible difficulties. The galleries of approach had fortunately not fallen after the fire-damp explosion; but the air was so heavy and so vitiated that more ventilators had to be installed. Every twenty minutes the pikemen relieved one another. They were advancing; scarcely two metres separated them from their mates. But now they worked feeling cold at their hearts, striking hard only out of vengeance; for the noises had ceased, and the low, clear cadence of the call no longer sounded. It was the twelfth day of their labours, the fifteenth since the catastrophe; and since the morning there had been a death-like silence.

The new accident increased the curiosity at Montsou, and the inhabitants organized excursions with such spirit that the Grégoires decided to follow the fashion. They arranged a party, and it was agreed that they should go to the Voreux in their carriage, while Madame Hennebeau took Lucie and Jeanne there in hers. Deneulin would show them over his yards and then they would return by Réquillart, where Négrel would tell them the exact state of things in the galleries, and if there was still hope. Finally, they would dine together in the evening.

When the Grégoires and their daughter Cécile arrived at the ruined mine, toward three o'clock, they found Madame Hennebeau already there, in a sea-blue dress, protecting herself under her parasol from the pale February sun. The warmth of spring was in the clear sky. M.

Hennebeau was there with Deneulin, and she was listening, with listless ear, to the account which the latter gave her of the efforts which had been made to dam up the canal. Jeanne, who always carried a sketch-book with her, began to draw, carried away by the horror of the subject; while Lucie, seated beside her on the remains of a wagon, was crying out with pleasure, and finding it awfully jolly. The incomplete dam allowed numerous leaks, and frothy streams fell in a cascade down the enormous hole of the engulfed mine. The crater was being emptied, however, and the water, drunk by the earth, was sinking, and revealing the fearful ruin at the bottom. Beneath the tender azure of this beautiful day there lay a sewer, the ruins of a town drowned and melted in mud.

"And people come out of their way to see that!" exclaimed M. Grégoire, disillusioned.

Cécile, rosy with health and glad to breathe so pure an air, was cheerfully joking, while Madame Hennebeau made a little grimace of repugnance as she murmured:

"The fact is, this is not pretty at all."

The two engineers laughed. They tried to interest the visitors, taking them round and explaining to them the working of the pumps and the manipulation of the stamper which drove in the piles. But the ladies became anxious. They shuddered when they knew that the pumps would have to work for six or seven years before the shaft was reconstructed and all the water exhausted from the mine. No, they would rather think of something else; this destruction was only good to give bad dreams.

"Let us go," said Madame Hennebeau, turning towards her carriage.

Lucie and Jeanne protested. What! so soon! and the drawing which was not finished. They wanted to remain; their father would bring them to dinner in the evening.

M. Hennebeau alone took his place with his wife in the carriage, for he wished to question Négrel.

"Very well! go on before," said M. Grégoire. "We will follow you; we have a little visit of five minutes to make over there at the settlement. Go on, go on! we shall be at Réquillart as soon as you."

He got up behind Madame Grégoire and Cécile, and while the other carriage went along by the canal, theirs gently ascended the slope.

Their excursion was to be completed by a visit of charity. Zacharie's death had filled them with pity for this tragical Maheu family, about whom the whole country was talking. They had no pity for the father, that brigand, that slayer of soldiers, who had to be struck down like a wolf. But the mother touched them, that poor woman who had just lost her son after having lost her husband, and whose daughter was perhaps a corpse beneath the earth; to say nothing of an invalid grandfather, a child who was lame as the result of a landslip, and a little girl who died of starvation during the strike. So that, though this family had in part deserved its misfortunes by the detestable spirit it had shown, they had resolved to assert the breadth of their charity, their desire for forgetfulness and conciliation, by themselves bringing an alms. Two parcels, carefully wrapped up, had been placed beneath a seat of the carriage.

An old woman pointed out to the coachman Maheude's house, No. 16 in the second block. But when the Grégoires alighted with the parcels, they knocked in vain; at last they struck their fists against the door, still without reply; the house echoed mournfully, like a house emptied by grief, frozen and dark, long since abandoned.

"There's no one there," said Cécile, disappointed. "What a nuisance! What shall we do with all this?"

Suddenly the door of the next house opened, and that Levaque woman appeared.

"Oh, sir! I beg pardon, ma'am. Excuse me, miss. It's the neighbour that you want? She's not there; she's at Réquillart."

With a flow of words she told them the story, repeating to them that people must help one another, and that she was keeping Lénore and Henri in her house to allow the mother to go and wait over there. Her eyes had fallen on the parcels, and she began to talk about her poor daughter, who had become a widow, displaying her own wretchedness, while her eyes shone with covetousness. Then, in a hesitating way, she muttered:

"I've got the key. If the lady and gentleman would really like — The grandfather is there."

The Grégoires looked at her in stupefaction. What! The grandfather was there! But no one had replied. He was sleeping, then? And when the Levaque made up her mind to open the door, what they saw stopped them on the threshold. Bonnemort was there alone, with large fixed eyes, nailed to his chair in front of the cold fireplace. Around him the room appeared larger without the clock or the polished deal furniture which formerly animated it; there only remained against the green crudity of the walls the portraits of the emperor and empress, whose rosy lips were smiling with official benevolence. The old man did not stir nor wink his eyelids beneath the sudden light from the door; he seemed imbecile, as though he had not seen all these people come in. At his feet lay his plate, garnished with ashes, such as is placed for cats for ordure.

"Don't mind if he's not very polite," said the Levaque woman, obligingly. "Seems he's broken something in his brain. It's a fortnight since he left off speaking."

But Bonnemort was shaken by some agitation, a deep scraping which seemed to arise from his belly, and he expectorated into the plate a thick black expectoration. The ashes were soaked into a coaly mud, all the coal of the mine which he drew from his chest. He had already resumed his immobility. He stirred no more, except at intervals, to spit.

Uneasy, and with stomachs turned, the Grégoires endeavoured to utter a few friendly and encouraging words.

"Well, my good man," said the father, "you have a cold, then?"

The old man, with his eyes to the wall, did not turn his head. And a heavy silence fell once more.

"They ought to make you a little gruel," added the mother.

He preserved his mute stiffness.

"I say, papa," murmured Cécile, "they certainly told us he was an invalid; only we did not think of it after-wards—"

She interrupted herself, much embar-rassed. After having placed on the table a pot-au-feu and two bottles of wine, she undid the second parcel and drew from it a pair of enormous boots. It was the present intended for the grandfather, and she held one boot in each hand, in confusion, contemplating the poor man's swollen feet, which would never walk more.

"Eh! they come a little late, don't they, my worthy fellow?" said M. Grégoire again, to enliven the situation. "It doesn't matter, they're always useful."

Bonnemort neither heard nor replied, with his terrible face as cold and as hard as a stone.

Then Cécile furtively placed the boots against the wall. But in spite of her precautions the nails clanked; and those enormous boots stood oppressively in the room.

"He won't say thank you," said the Levaque woman, who had cast a look of deep envy on the boots. "Might as well give a pair of spectacles to a duck, asking your pardon."

She went on; she was trying to draw the Grégoires into her own house, where she hoped to gain their pity. At last she thought of a pretext; she praised Henri and Lénore, who were so good, so gentle, and so intelligent, answering like angels the questions that they were asked. They would tell the lady and gentleman all that they wished to know.

"Will you come for a moment, my child?" asked the father, glad to get away.

"Yes, I'll follow you," she replied.

Cécile remained alone with Bonnemort. What kept her there trembling and fascinated, was the thought that she seemed to recognize this old man: where then had she met this square livid face, tattoed with coal? Suddenly she remembered; she saw again a mob of shouting people who surrounded her, and she felt cold hands pressing her neck. It was he; she saw the man again; she looked at his hands placed on his knees, the hands of an invalid workman whose whole strength is in his wrists, still firm in spite of age. Gradually Bonnemort seemed to awake, he perceived her and examined her in his turn. A flame mounted to his cheeks, a nervous spasm drew his mouth, from which flowed a thin streak of black saliva. Fascinated, they remained opposite each other – she flourishing, plump, and fresh from the long idleness and sated comfort of her race; he swollen with water, with the pitiful ugliness of a foundered beast, destroyed from father to son by a century of work and hunger.

At the end of ten minutes, when the Grégoires, surprised at not seeing Cécile, came back into the Maheus' house, they uttered a terrible cry. Their daughter was lying on the ground, with livid face, strangled. At her neck fingers had left the red imprint of a giant's hand. Bonnemort, tottering on his dead legs, had fallen beside her without power to rise. His hands were still hooked, and he looked round with his imbecile air and large open eyes. In his fall he had broken his plate, the ashes were spread round, the mud of the black expectoration had stained the floor; while the great pair of boots, safe and sound, stood side by side against the wall.

It was never possible to establish the exact facts. Why had Cécile come near? How could Bonnemort, nailed to his chair, have been able to seize her throat? Evidently, when he held her, he must have become furious, constantly pressing, overthrown with her, and stifling her cries to the last groan. Not a sound, not a moan had traversed the thin partition to the neighbouring house. It seemed to be an outbreak of sudden madness, a longing to murder before this white young neck. Such savagery was stupefying in an old invalid, who had lived like a worthy man, an obedient brute, opposed to new ideas. What rancour, unknown to himself, by some slow process of poisoning, had risen from his bowels to his brain? The horror of it led to the conclusion that he was unconscious, that it was the crime of an idiot.

The Grégoires, meanwhile, on their knees, were sobbing, choked with grief. Their idolized daughter, that daughter desired so long, on whom they had lavished all their goods, whom they used to watch sleeping, on tiptoe, whom they never thought sufficiently well nourished, never sufficiently plump! It was the downfall of their very life; what was the good of living, now that they would have to live without her?

The Levaque woman in distraction cried:

"Ah, the old beggar! what's he done there? Who would have expected such a thing? And Maheude, who won't come back till evening! Shall I go and fetch her?"

The father and mother were crushed, and did not reply.

"Eh? It will be better. I'll go."

But, before going, the Levaque woman looked at the boots. The whole settlement was excited, and a crowd was already hustling around. Perhaps they would get stolen. And then the Maheus had no man, now, to put them on. She quietly carried them away. They would just fit Bouteloup's feet.

At Réquillart the Hennebeaus, with Négrel, waited a long time for the Grégoires. Négrel, who had come up from the pit, gave details. They hoped to communicate that very evening with the prisoners, but they-would certainly find nothing but corpses, for the death-like silence continued. Behind the engineer, Maheude, seated on the beam, was listening with white face, when the Levaque woman came up and told her the old man's strange deed. And she only made a sweeping gesture of impatience and irritation. She followed her, however.

Madame Hennebeau was much affected. What an abomination! That poor Cécile, so merry that very day, so full of life an hour before! M. Hennebeau had to lead his wife for a moment into old Mouque's hovel. With his awkward hands he unfastened her dress, troubled by the odour of musk which her open bodice exhaled. And as with streaming tears she clasped Négrel, terrified at this death which cut short the marriage, the husband watched them lamenting together, and was delivered from one anxiety. This misfortune would arrange everything; he preferred to keep his nephew for fear of his coachman.

Chapter 5

AT the bottom of the shaft the abandoned wretches were yelling with terror. The water now came up to their hips. The noise of the torrent dazed them, the final falling in of the tubbing sounded like the last crack of doom; and their bewilderment was completed by the neighing of the horses shut up in the stable, the terrible, unforgettable death-cry of an animal that is being slaughtered.

Mouque had let go Bataille. The old horse was there, trembling, with its dilated eye fixed on this water which was constantly rising. The pit-eye was rapidly filling; the greenish flood slowly enlarged under the red gleam of the three lamps which were still burning under the roof. And suddenly, when he felt this ice soaking his coat, he set out in a furious gallop, and was engulfed and lost at the end of one of the haulage galleries.

Then there was a general rush, the men following the beast.

"Nothing more to be done in this damned hole!" shouted Mouque. "We must try at Réquillart."

The idea that they might get out by the old neighbouring pit if they arrived before the passage was cut off, now carried them away. The twenty hustled one another as they went in single file, holding their lamps in the air so that the water should not extinguish them. Fortunately, the gallery rose with an imperceptible slope, and they proceeded for two hundred metres, struggling against the flood, which was not now gaining on them. Sleeping beliefs reawakened in these distracted souls; they invoked the earth, for it was the earth that was avenging herself, discharging the blood from the vein because they had cut one of her arteries. An old man stammered forgotten prayers, bending his thumbs backwards to appease the evil spirits of the mine.

But at the first turning disagreement broke out; the groom proposed turning to the left, others declared that they could make a short cut by going to the right. A minute was lost.

"Well, die there! what the devil does it matter to me?" Chaval brutally exclaimed. "I go this way."

He turned to the right, and two mates followed him. The others continued to rush behind Father Mouque, who had grown up at the bottom of Réquillart. He himself hesitated, however, not knowing where to turn. They lost their heads; even the old men could no longer recognize the passages, which lay like a tangled skein before them. At every bifurcation they were pulled up short by uncertainty, and yet they had to decide.

Étienne was running last, delayed by Catherine, who was paralysed by fatigue and fear. He would have gone to the right with Chaval, for he thought that the better road; but he had not, preferring to part from Chaval. The rush continued, however; some of the mates had gone from their side, and only seven were left behind old Mouque.

"Hang on to my neck and I will carry you," said Étienne to the young girl, seeing her grow weak.

"No, let me be," she murmured. "I can't do more; I would rather die at once."

They delayed and were left fifty metres behind; he was lifting her, in spite of her resistance, when the gallery was suddenly stopped up; an enormous block fell in and separated them from the others. The inundation was already soaking the soil, which was shifting on every side. They had to retrace their steps; then they no longer knew in what direction they were going. There was an end of all hope of escaping by Réquillart. Their only remaining hope was to gain the upper workings, from which they might perhaps be delivered if the water sank.

Étienne at last recognized the Guillaume seam.

"Good!" he exclaimed. "Now I know where we are. By God! we were in the right road; but we may go to the devil now! Here, let us go straight on; we will climb up the passage."

The flood was beating against their breasts, and they walked very slowly. As long as they had light they did not despair, and they blew out one of the lamps to economize the oil, meaning to empty it into the other lamp. They had reached the chimney passage, when a noise behind made them turn. Was it some mates, then, who had also found the road barred and were returning? A roaring sound came from afar; they could not understand this tempest which approached them, spattering foam. And they cried out when they saw a gigantic whitish mass coming out of the shadow and trying to rejoin them between the narrow timbering in which it was being crushed.

It was Bataille. On leaving the pit-eye he had wildly galloped along the dark galleries. He seemed to know his road in this subterranean town which he had inhabited for eleven years, and his eyes saw clearly in the depths of the eternal night in which he had lived. He galloped on and on, bending his head, drawing up his feet, passing through these narrow tubes in the earth, filled by his great body. Road succeeded to road,. and the forked turnings were passed without any hesitation. Where was he going? Over there, perhaps, towards that vision of his youth, to the mill where he had been born on the bank of the Scarpe, to the confused recollection of the sun burning in the air like a great lamp. He desired to live, his beast's memory awoke; the longing to breathe once more the air of the plains drove him straight onwards to the discovery of that hole, the exit beneath the warm sun into light. Rebellion carried away his ancient resignation; this pit was murdering him after having blinded him. The water which pursued him was lashing him on the flanks and biting him on the crupper. But as he went deeper in, the galleries became narrower, the roofs lower, and the walls protruded. He galloped on in spite of everything, grazing himself, leaving shreds of his limbs on the timber. From every side the mine seemed to be pressing on to him to take him and to stifle him.

Then Étienne and Catherine, as he came near them, perceived that he was strangling between the rocks. He had stumbled and broken his two front legs. With a last effort, he dragged himself a few metres, but his flanks could not pass; he remained hemmed in and garrotted by the earth. With his bleeding head stretched out, he still sought for some crack with his great troubled eyes.

The water was rapidly covering him; he began to neigh with that terrible prolonged death-rattle with which the other horses had already died in the stable. It was a sight of fearful agony, this old beast shattered and motionless, struggling at this depth, far from the daylight. The flood was drowning his mane, and his cry of distress never ceased; he uttered it more hoarsely, with his large open mouth stretched out. There was a last rumble, the hollow sound of a cask which is being filled; then deep silence fell.

"Oh, my God! take me away!" Catherine sobbed. "Ah, my God! I'm afraid; I don't want to die. Take me away! take me away!"

She had seen death. The fallen shaft, the inundated mine, nothing had seized her with such terror as this clamour of Bataille in agony. And she constantly heard it; her ears were ringing with it; all her flesh was shuddering with it.

"Take me away! take me away!"

Étienne had seized her and lifted her; it was, indeed, time. They ascended the chimney passage, soaked to the shoulders. He was obliged to help her, for she had no strength to cling to the timber. Three times over he thought that she was slipping from him and falling back into that deep sea of which the tide was roaring beneath them. However, they were able to breathe for a few minutes when they reached the first gallery, which was still free. The water reappeared, and they had to hoist themselves up again. And for hours this ascent continued, the flood chasing them from passage to passage, and constantly forcing them to ascend. At the sixth level a respite rendered them feverish with hope, and it seemed that the waters were becoming stationary. But a more rapid rise took place, and they had to climb to the seventh and then to the eighth level. Only one remained, and when they had reached it they anxiously watched each centimetre by which the water gained on them. If it did not stop they would then die like the old horse, crushed against the roof, and their chests filled by the flood.

Landslips echoed every moment. The whole mine was shaken, and its distended bowels burst with the enormous flood which gorged them. At the end of the galleries the air, driven back, pressed together and crushed, exploding terribly amid split rocks and overthrown soil. It was a terrifying uproar of interior cataclysms, a remnant of the ancient battle when deluges overthrew the earth, burying the mountains beneath the plains.

And Catherine, shaken and dazed by this continuous downfall, joined her hands, stammering the same words without cessation:

"I don't want to die! I don't want to die!"

To reassure her, Étienne declared that the water was not now moving. Their flight had lasted for fully six hours, and they would soon be rescued. He said six hours without knowing, for they had lost all count of time. In reality, a whole day had already passed in their climb up through the Guillaume seam.

Drenched and shivering, they settled themselves down. She undressed herself without shame and wrung out her clothes, then she put on again the jacket and breeches, and let them finish drying on her. As her feet were bare, he made her take his own sabots. They could wait patiently now; they had lowered the wick of the lamp, leaving only the feeble gleam of a night-light. But their stomachs were torn by cramp, and they both realized that they were dying of hunger. Up till now they had not felt that they were living. The catastrophe had occurred before breakfast, and now they found their bread-and-butter swollen by the water and changed into sop. She had to become angry before he would accept his share. As soon as she had eaten she fell asleep from weariness, on the cold earth. He was devoured by insomnia, and watched over her with fixed eyes and forehead between his hands.

How many hours passed by thus? He would have been unable to say. All that he knew was that before him, through the hole they had ascended, he had seen the flood reappear, black and moving, the beast whose back was ceaselessly swelling out to reach them. At first it was only a thin line, a supple serpent stretching itself out; then it enlarged into a crawling, crouching flank; and soon it reached them, and the sleeping girl's feet were touched by it. In his anxiety he yet hesitated to wake her. Was it not cruel to snatch her from this repose of unconscious ignorance, which was, perhaps, lulling her with a dream of the open air and of life beneath the sun? Besides, where could they fly? And he thought and remembered that the upbrow established at this part of the seam communicated end to end with that which served the upper level. That would be a way out. He let her sleep as long as possible, watching the flood gain on them, waiting for it to chase them away. At last he lifted her gently, and a great shudder passed over her.

"Ah, my God! it's true! it's beginning again, my God!" She remembered, she cried out, again finding death so near.

"No! calm yourself," he whispered. "We can pass, upon my word!"

To reach the upbrow they had to walk doubled up, again wetted to the shoulders. And the climbing began anew, now more dangerous, through this hole entirely of timber, a hundred metres long. At first they wished to pull the cable so as to fix one of the carts at the bottom, for if the other should come down during their ascent, they would be crushed. But nothing moved, some obstacle interfered with the mechanism. They ventured in, not daring to make use of the cable which was in their way, and tearing their nails against the smooth framework. He came behind, supporting her by his head when she slipped with torn hands. Suddenly they came across the splinters of a beam which barred the way. A portion of the soil had fallen down and prevented them form going any higher. Fortunately a door opened here and they passed into a passage. They were stupefied to see the flicker of a lamp in front of them. A man cried wildly to them:

"More clever people as big fools as I am!"

They recognized Chaval, who had found himself blocked by the landslip which filled the upbrow; his two mates who had set out with him had been left on the way with fractured skulls. He was wounded in the elbow, but had had the courage to go back on his knees, take their lamps, and search them to steal their bread-and-butter. As he escaped, a final downfall behind his back had closed the gallery.

He immediately swore that he would not share his victuals with these people who came up out of the earth. He would sooner knock their brains out. Then he, too, recognized them; his anger fell, and he began to laugh with a laugh of evil joy.

"Ah! it's you, Catherine! you've come a cropper, and you want to join your man again. Well, well! we'll play out the game together."

He pretended not to see Étienne. The latter, overwhelmed by this encounter, made a gesture as though to protect the putter, who was pressing herself against him. He must, however, accept the situation. Speaking as though they had left each other good friends an hour before, he simply asked:

"Have you looked down below? We can't pass through the cuttings, then?"

Chaval still grinned.

"Ah. bosh! the cuttings! They've fallen in too; we are between two walls, a real mousetrap. But you can go back by the brow if you are a good diver."

The water, in fact, was rising; they could hear it rippling. Their retreat was already cut off. And he was right; it was a mousetrap, a gallery-end obstructed before and behind by considerable falls of earth. There was not one issue; all three were walled up.

"Then you'll stay?" Chaval added, jeeringly. "Well, it's the best you can do, and if you'll just leave me alone, I shan't even speak to you. There's still room here for two men. We shall soon see which will die first, provided they don't come to us, which seems a tough job."

The young man said:

"If we were to hammer, they would hear us, perhaps." "I'm tired of hammering. Here, try yourself with this stone."

Étienne picked up the fragment of sandstone which the other had already broken off, and against the seam at the end he struck the miner's call, the prolonged roll by which workmen in peril signal their presence. Then he placed his ear to listen. Twenty times over he persisted; no sound replied.

During this time Chaval affected to be coolly attending to his little household. First he arranged the three lamps against the wall; only one was burning, the others could be used later on. Afterwards, he placed on a piece of timber the two slices of bread-and-butter which were still left. That was the sideboard; he could last quite two days with that, if he were careful. He turned round saying:

"You know, Catherine, there will be half for you when you are famished."

The young girl was silent. It completed her unhappiness to find herself again between these two men.

And their awful life began. Neither Chaval nor Étienne opened their mouths, seated on the earth a few paces from each other. At a hint from the former the latter extinguished his lamp, a piece of useless luxury; then they sank back into silence. Catherine was lying down near Étienne, restless under the glances of her former lover. The hours passed by; they heard the low murmur of the water for ever rising; while from time to time deep shocks and distant echoes announced the final settling down of the mine. When the lamp was empty and they had to open another to light it, they were, for a moment, disturbed by the fear of fire-damp; but they would rather have been blown up at once than live on in darkness. Nothing exploded, however; there was no fire-damp. They stretched themselves out again, and the hours continued to pass by.

A noise aroused Étienne and Catherine, and they raised their heads. Chaval had decided to eat; he had cut off half a slice of bread-and-butter, and was chewing it slowly, to avoid the temptation of swallowing it all. They gazed at him, tortured by hunger.

"Well, do you refuse?" he said to the putter, in his provoking way. "You're wrong."

She had lowered her eyes, fearing to yield; her stomach was torn by such cramps that tears were swelling beneath her eyelids. But she understood what he was asking; in the morning he had breathed over her neck; he was seized again by one of his old furies of desire on seeing her near the other man. The glances with which he called her had a flame in them which she knew well, the flame of his crises of jealousy when he would fall on her with his fists, accusing her of committing abominations with her mother's lodger. And she was not willing; she trembled lest, by returning to him, she should throw these two men on to each other in this narrow cave, where they were all in agony together. Good

God! why could they not end together in comradeship!

Étienne would have died of inanition rather than beg a mouthful of bread from Chaval. The silence became heavy; an eternity seemed to be prolonging itself with the slowness of monotonous minutes which passed by, one by one, without hope. They had now been shut up together for a day. The second lamp was growing pale, and they lighted the third.

Chaval started on his second slice of bread-and-butter, and growled:

"Come then, stupid!"

Catherine shivered. Étienne had turned away in order to leave her free. Then, as she did not stir, he said to her in a low voice:

"Go, my child."

The tears which she was stifling then rushed forth. She wept for a long time, without even strength to rise, no longer knowing if she was hungry, suffering with pain which she felt all over her body. He was standing up, going backward and forwards, vainly beating the miners call, enraged at this remainder of life which he was obliged to live here tied to a rival whom he detested. Not even enough space to die away from each other! As soon as he had gone ten paces he must come back and knock up against this man. And she, this sorrowful girl whom they were disputing over even in the earth! She would belong to the one who lived longest; that man would steal her from him should he go first. There was no end to it; the hours followed the hours; the revolting promiscuity became worse, with the poison of their breaths and the ordure of their necessities satisfied in common. Twice he rushed against the rocks as though to open them with his fists.

Another day was done, and Chaval had seated himself near Catherine, sharing with her his last half-slice. She was chewing the mouthfuls painfully; he made her pay for each with a caress, in his jealous obstinacy not willing to die until he had had her again in the other man's presence. She abandoned herself in exhaustion. But when he tried to take her she complained.

"Oh, let me be! you're breaking my bones."

Étienne, with a shudder, had placed his forehead against the timber so as not to see. He came back with a wild leap

"Let her be, by God!"

"Does it concern you?" said Chaval. "She's my woman; I suppose she belongs to me!"

And he took her again and pressed her, out of bravado, crushing his red moustache against her mouth, and continuing:

"Will you leave us alone, eh? Will you be good enough to look over there if we are at it?"

But Étienne, with white lips, shouted:

"If you don't let her go, I'll do for you!"

The other quickly stood up, for he had understood by the hiss of the voice that his mate was in earnest. Death seemed to them too slow; it was necessary that one of them should immediately yield his place. It was the old battle beginning over again, down in the earth where they would soon sleep side by side; and they had so little room that they could not swing their fists without grazing them.

"Look out!" growled Chaval. "This time I'll have you."

From that moment Étienne became mad. His eyes seemed drowned in red vapour, his chest was congested by the flow of blood. The need to kill seized him irresistibly, a physical need, like the irritation of mucus which causes a violent spasm of coughing. It rose and broke out beyond his will, beneath the pressure of the hereditary disease. He had seized a sheet of slate in the wall and he shook it and tore it out, a very large, heavy piece. Then with both hands and with tenfold strength he brought it down on Chaval's skull.

The latter had not time to jump backwards. He fell, his face crushed, his skull broken. The brains had be-spattered the roof of the gallery, and a purple jet flowed from the wound, like the continuous jet of a spring. Immediately there was a pool, which reflected the smoky star of the lamp. Darkness was invading the walled-up cave, and this body, lying on the earth, looked like the black boss of a mass of rough coal.

Leaning over, with wide eyes, Étienne looked at him. It was done, then; he had killed. All his struggles came back to his memory confusedly, that useless fight against the poison which slept in his muscles, the slowly accumulated alcohol of his race. He was, however, only intoxicated by hunger; the remote intoxication of his parents had been enough. His hair stood up before the horror of this murder; and yet, in spite of the revolt which came from his education, a certain gladness made his heart beat, the animal joy of an appetite at length satisfied. He felt pride, too, the pride of the stronger man. The little soldier appeared before him, with his throat opened by a knife, killed by a child. Now he, too, had killed.

But Catherine, standing erect, uttered a loud cry:

"My God! he is dead!"

"Are you sorry?" asked Étienne, fiercely.

She was choking, she stammered. Then, tottering. she threw herself into his arms.

"Ah, kill me too! Ah, let us both die!"

She clasped him, hanging to his shoulders, and he clasped her; and they hoped that they would die. But death was in no hurry, and they unlocked their arms. Then, while she hid her eyes, he dragged away the wretch, and threw him down the upbrow, to remove him from the narrow space in which they still had to live. Life would no longer have been possible with that corpse beneath their feet. And they were terrified when they heard it plunge into the midst of the foam which leapt up. The water had already filled that hole, then? They saw it; it was entering the gallery.

Then there was a new struggle. They had lighted the last lamp; it was becoming exhausted in illuminating this flood, with its regular, obstinate rise which never ceased. At first the water came up to their ankles; then it wetted their knees. The passage sloped up, and they took refuge at the end. This gave them a respite for some hours. But the flood caught them up, and bathed them to the waist. Standing up, brought to bay, with their spines close against the rock, they watched it ever and ever increasing. When it reached their mouths, all would be over. The lamp, which they had fastened up, threw a yellow light on the rapid surge of the little waves. It was becoming pale; they could distinguish no more than a constantly diminishing semicircle, as though eaten away by the darkness which seemed to grow with the flood; and suddenly the darkness enveloped them.

The lamp had gone out, after having spat forth its last drop of oil. There was now complete and absolute night, that night of the earth which they would have to sleep through without ever again opening their eyes to the brightness of the sun.

"By God!" Étienne swore, in a low voice.

Catherine, as though she had felt the darkness seize her, sheltered herself against him. She repeated, in a whisper, the miner's saying:

"Death is blowing out the lamp."

Yet in the face of this threat their instincts struggled, the fever for life animated them. He violently set himself to hollow out the slate with the hook of the lamp, while she helped him with her nails. They formed a sort of elevated bench, and when they had both hoisted themselves up to it, they found themselves seated with hanging legs and bent backs, for the vault forced them to lower their heads. They now only felt the icy water at their heels; but before long the cold was at their ankles, their calves, their knees, with its invincible, truceless movement. The bench, not properly smoothed, was soaked in moisture, and so slippery that they had to hold themselves on vigorously to avoid slipping off. It was the end; what could they expect, reduced to this niche where they dared not move, exhausted, starving, having neither bread nor light? and they suffered especially from the darkness, which would not allow them to see the coming of death. There was deep silence; the mine, being gorged with water, no longer stirred. They had nothing beneath them now but the sensation of that sea, swelling out its silent tide from the depths of the galleries.

The hours succeeded one another, all equally black; but they were not able to measure their exact duration, becoming more and more vague in their calculation of time. Their tortures, which might have been expected to lengthen the minutes, rapidly bore them away. They thought that they had only been shut up for two days and a night, when in reality the third day had already come to an end. All hope of help had gone; no one knew they were there, no one could come down to them. And hunger would finish them off if the inundation spared them. For one last time it occurred to them to beat the call, but the stone was lying beneath the water. Besides, who would hear them?

Catherine was leaning her aching head against the seam, when she sat up with a start.

"Listen!" she said.

At first Étienne thought she was speaking of the low noise of the ever-rising water. He lied in order to quiet her.

"It's me you hear; I'm moving my legs."

"No, no; not that! Over there, listen!"

And she placed her ear to the coal. He understood, and did likewise. They waited for some seconds, with stifled breath. Then, very far away and very weak, they heard three blows at long intervals. But they still doubted; their ears were ringing; perhaps it was the cracking of the soil. And they knew not what to strike with in answer.

Étienne had an idea.

"You have the sabots. Take them off and strike with the heels."

She struck, beating the miner's call; and they listened and again distinguished the three blows far off. Twenty times over they did it, and twenty times the blows replied. They wept and embraced each other, at the risk of losing their balance. At last the mates were there, they were coming. An overflowing joy and love carried away the torments of expectation and the rage of their vain appeals, as though their rescuers had only to split the rock with a finger to deliver them.

"Eh!" she cried merrily; "wasn't it lucky that I leant my head?"

"Oh, you've got an ear!" he said in his turn. "Now, *I* heard nothing."

From that moment they relieved each other, one of them always listening, ready to answer at the least signal. They soon caught the sounds of the pick; the work of approaching them was beginning, a gallery was being opened. Not a sound escaped them. But their joy sank. In vain they laughed to deceive each other; despair was gradually seizing them. At first they entered into long explanations; evidently they were being approached from Réquillart. The gallery descended in the bed; perhaps several were being opened, for there were always three men hewing. Then they talked less, and were at last silent when they came to calculate the enormous mass which separated them from their mates. They continued their reflections in silence, counting the days and days that a workman would take to penetrate such a block. They would never be reached soon enough; they would have time to die twenty times over. And no longer venturing to exchange a word in this redoubled anguish, they gloomily replied to the appeals by a roll of the sabots, without hope, only retaining the mechanical need to tell the others that they were still alive.

Thus passed a day, two days. They had been at the bottom six days. The water had stopped at their knees, neither rising nor falling, and their legs seemed to be melting away in this icy bath. They could certainly keep them out for an hour or so, but their position then became so uncomfortable that they were twisted by horrible cramps, and were obliged to let their feet fall in again. Every ten minutes they hoisted themselves back by a jerk on the slippery rock. The fractures of the coal struck into their spines, and they felt at the back of their necks a fixed intense pain, through having to keep constantly bent in order to avoid striking their heads. And their suffocation increased; the air, driven back by the water, was compressed into a sort of bell in which they were shut up. Their voices were muffled, and seemed to come from afar. Their ears began to buzz, they heard the peals of a furious tocsin, the tramp of a flock beneath a storm of hail, going on unceasingly.

At first Catherine suffered horribly from hunger. She pressed her poor shrivelled hands against her breasts, her breathing was deep and hollow, a continuous tearing moan, as though tongs were tearing her stomach.

Étienne, choked by the same torture, was feeling feverishly round him in the darkness, when his fingers came upon a half-rotten piece of timber, which his nails could crumble. He gave a handful of it to the putter, who swallowed it greedily. For two days they lived on this worm-eaten wood, devouring it all, in despair when it was finished, grazing their hands in the effort to crush the other planks which were still solid with resisting fibres. Their torture increased, and they were enraged that they could not chew the cloth of their clothes. A leather belt, which he wore round the waist, relieved them a little. He bit small pieces from it with his teeth, and she chewed them, and endeavoured to swallow them. This occupied their jaws, and gave them the illusion of eating. Then, when the belt was finished, they went back to their clothes, sucking them for hours.

But soon these violent crises subsided; hunger became only a low deep ache with the slow progressive languor of their strength. No doubt they would have succumbed if they had not had as much water as they desired. They merely bent down and drank from the hollow of the hand, and that very frequently, parched by a thirst which all this water could not quench.

On the seventh day Catherine was bending down to drink, when her hand struck some floating body before her.

"I say, look! What's this?"

Étienne felt in the darkness.

"I can't make out; it seems like the cover of a ventilation door."

She drank, but as she was drawing up a second mouthful the body came back, striking her hand. And she uttered a terrible cry.

"My God! it's he!"

"Whom do you mean?"

"Him! You know well enough. I felt his moustache." It was Chaval's corpse, risen from the upbrow and pushed on to them by the flow. Étienne stretched out his arm; he, too, felt the moustache and the crushed nose, and shuddered with disgust and fear. Seized by horrible nausea, Catherine had spat out the water which was still in her mouth. It seemed to her that she had been drinking blood, and that all the deep water before her was now that man's blood.

"Wait!" stammered Étienne. "I'll push him off!"

He kicked the corpse, which moved off. But soon they felt it again striking against their legs.

"By God! Get off!"

And the third time Étienne had to leave it. Some current always brought it back. Chaval would not go; he desired to be with them, against them. It was an awful companion, at last poisoning the air. All that day they never drank, struggling, preferring to die. It was not until the next day that their suffering decided them: they pushed away the body at each mouthful and drank in spite of it. It had not been worth while to knock his brains out, for he came back between him and her, obstinate in his jealousy. To the very end he would be there, even though he was dead, preventing them from coming together.

A day passed, and again another day. At every shiver of the water Étienne perceived a slight blow from the man he had killed, the simple elbowing of a neighbour who is reminding you of his presence. And every time it came he shuddered. He continually saw it there, swollen, greenish, with the red moustache and the crushed face. Then he no longer remembered; he had not killed him; the other man was swimming and trying to bite him.

Catherine was now shaken by long endless fits of crying, after which she was completely prostrated. She fell at last into a condition of irresistible drowsiness. He would arouse her, but she stammered a few words and at once fell asleep again without even raising her eyelids; and fearing lest she should be drowned, he put his arm round her waist. It was he now who replied to the mates. The blows of the pick were now approaching, he could hear them behind his back. But his strength, too, was diminishing; he had lost all courage to strike. They were known to be there; why weary oneself more? It no longer interested him whether they came or not. In the stupefaction of waiting he would forget for hours at a time what he was waiting for.

One relief comforted them a little: the water sank, and Chaval's body moved off. For nine days the work of their deliverance had been going on, and they were for the first time taking a few steps in the gallery when a fearful commotion threw them to the ground. They felt for each other and remained in each other's arms like mad people, not understanding, thinking the catastrophe was beginning over again. Nothing more stirred, the sound of the picks had ceased.

In the corner where they were seated holding each other, side by side, a low laugh came from Catherine.

"It must be good outside. Come, let's go out of here." Étienne at first struggled against this madness. But the contagion was shaking his stronger head, and he lost the exact sensation of reality. All their senses seemed to go astray, especially Catherine's. She was shaken by fever, tormented now by the need to talk and move. The ringing in her ears had become the murmur of flowing water, the song of birds; she smelled the strong odour of crushed grass, and could see clearly great yellow patches floating before her eyes, so large that she thought she was out of doors, near the canal, in the meadows on a fine summer day.

"Eh? how warm it is! Take me, then; let us keep together. Oh, always, always!"

He pressed her, and she rubbed herself against him for a long time, continuing to chatter like a happy girl:

"How silly we have been to wait so long! I would have liked you at once, and you did not understand; you sulked. Then, do you remember, at our house at night, when we could not sleep, with our faces out listening to each other's breathing, with such a longing to come together?"

He was won by her gaiety, and joked over the recollection of their silent tenderness.

"You struck me once. Yes, yes, blows on both cheeks!"

"It was because I loved you," she murmured. "You see, I prevented myself from thinking of you. I said to myself that it was quite done with, and all the time I knew that one day or another we should get together. It only wanted an opportunity – some lucky chance. Wasn't it so?"

A shudder froze him. He tried to shake off this dream; then he repeated slowly:

"Nothing is ever done with; a little happiness is enough to make everything begin again."

"Then you'll keep me, and it will be all right this time?"

And she slipped down fainting. She was so weak that her low voice died out. In terror he kept her against his heart.

"Are you in pain?"

She sat up surprised.

"No, not at all. Why?"

But this question aroused her from her dream. She gazed at the darkness with distraction, wringing her hands in another fit of sobbing.

"My God, my God, how black it is!"

It was no longer the meadows, the odour of the grass, the song of larks, the great yellow sun; it was the fallen, inundated mine, the stinking gloom, the melancholy dripping of this cellar where they had been groaning for so many days. Her perverted senses now increased the horror of it; her childish superstitions came back to her; she saw the Black Man, the old dead miner who returns to the pit to twist naughty girls' necks.

"Listen! did you hear?"

"No, nothing; I heard nothing."

"Yes, the Man – you know? Look! he is there. The earth has let all the blood out of the vein to revenge itself for being cut into; and he is there – you can see him – look! blacker than night. Oh, I'm so afraid, I'm so afraid!"

She became silent, shivering. Then in a very low voice she whispered:

"No, it's always the other one."

"What other one?"

"Him who is with us; who is not alive."

The image of Chaval haunted her, she talked of him confusedly, she described the dog's life she led with him, the only day when he had been kind to her at Jean-Bart, the other days of follies and blows, when he would kill her with caresses after having covered her with kicks.

"I tell you that he's coming, that he will still keep us from being together! His jealousy is coming on him again. Oh, push him off! Oh, keep me close!"

With a sudden impulse she hung on to him, seeking his mouth and pressing her own passionately to it. The darkness lighted up, she saw the sun again, and she laughed a quiet laugh of love. He shuddered to feel her thus against his flesh, half naked beneath the tattered jacket and trousers, and he seized her with a reawakening of his virility. It was at length their wedding night, at the bottom of this tomb, on this bed of mud, the longing not to die before they had had their happiness, the obstinate longing to live and make life one last time. They loved each other in despair of everything, in death.

After that there was nothing more. Étienne was seated on the ground, always in the same corner, and Catherine was lying motionless on his knees. Hours and hours passed by. For a long time he thought she was sleeping; then he touched her; she was very cold, she was dead. He did not move, however, for fear of arousing her. The idea that he was the first who had possessed her as a woman, and that she might be pregnant, filled him with tenderness. Other ideas, the desire to go away with her, joy at what they would both do later on, came to him at moments, but so vaguely that it seemed only as though his forehead had been touched by a breath of sleep. He grew weaker, he only had strength to make a little gesture, a slow movement of the hand, to assure himself that she was certainly there, like a sleeping child in her frozen stiffness. Everything was being annihilated; the night itself had disappeared, and he was nowhere, out of space, out of time. Something was certainly striking beside his head, violent blows were approaching him; but he had been too lazy to reply, benumbed by immense fatigue; and now he knew nothing, he only dreamed that she was walking before him, and that he heard the slight clank of her sabots. Two days passed; she had not stirred; he touched her with his mechanical gesture, reassured to find her so quiet.

Étienne felt a shock. Voices were sounding, rocks were rolling to his feet. When he perceived a lamp he wept. His blinking eyes followed the light, he was never tired of looking at it, enraptured by this reddish point which scarcely stained the darkness. But some mates carried him away, and he allowed them to introduce some spoonfuls of soup between his clenched teeth. It was only in the Réquillart gallery that he recognized someone standing before him, the engineer, Négrel; and these two men, with their contempt for each other – the rebellious workman and the sceptical master – threw themselves on each other's necks, sobbing loudly in the deep upheaval of all the humanity within them. It was an immense sadness, the misery of generations, the extremity of grief into which life can fall.

At the surface, Maheude, stricken down near dead Catherine, uttered a cry, then another, then another – very long, deep, incessant moans. Several corpses had already been brought up, and placed in a row on the ground: Chaval, who was thought to have been crushed beneath a landslip. a trammer, and two hewers, also crushed, with brainless skulls and bellies swollen with water. Women in the crowd went out of their minds, tearing their skirts and scratching their faces. When Étienne was at last taken out, after having been accustomed to the lamps and fed a little, he appeared fleshless, and his hair was quite white. People turned away and shuddered at this old man. Maheude left off crying to stare at him stupidly with her large fixed eyes.

Chapter 6

IT was four o'clock in the morning, and the fresh April night was growing warm at the approach of day. In the limpid sky the stars were twinkling out, while the east grew purple with dawn. And a slight shudder passed over the drowsy black country, the vague rumour which precedes awakening.

Étienne, with long strides, was following the Vandame road. He had just passed six weeks at Montsou, in bed at the hospital. Though very thin and yellow, he felt strength to go, and he went. The Company, still trembling for its pits, was constantly sending men away, and had given him notice that he could not be kept on. He was offered the sum of one hundred francs, with the paternal advice to leave off working in mines, as it would now be too severe for him. But he refused the hundred francs. He had already received a letter from Pluchart, calling him to Paris, and enclosing money for the journey. His old dream would be realized.

The night before, on leaving the hospital, he had slept at the Bon-Joyeux, Widow Désir's. And he rose early; only one desire was left, to bid his mates farewell before taking the eight o'clock train at Marchiennes.

For a moment Étienne stopped on the road, which was now becoming rose-coloured. It was good to breathe that pure air of the precocious spring. It would turn out a superb day. The sun was slowly rising, and the life of the earth was rising with it. And he set out walking again, vigorously striking with his dogwood stick, watching the plain afar, as it rose from the vapours of the night. He had seen no one; Maheude had come once to the hospital, and, probably, had not been able to come again. But he knew that the whole settlement of the Deux-Cent-Quarante was now going down at Jean-Bart, and that she too had taken work there. Little by little the deserted roads were peopled, and colliers constantly passed Étienne with pallid, silent faces. The Company, people said, was abusing its victory. After two and a half months of strike, when they had returned to the pits, conquered by hunger, they had been obliged to accept the timbering tariff, that disguised decrease in wages, now the more hateful because stained with the blood of their mates. They were being robbed of an hour's work, they were being made false to their oath never to submit; and this imposed perjury stuck in their throats like gall. Work was beginning again everywhere, at Mirou, at Madeleine, at Crévecoeur, at the Victoire. Everywhere, in the morning haze, along the roads lost in darkness, the flock was tramping on, rows of men trotting with faces bent towards the earth, like cattle led to the slaughter-house. They shivered beneath their thin garments, folding their arms, rolling their hips, expanding their backs with the humps formed by the brick between the shirt and the jacket. And in this wholesale return to work, in these mute shadows, all black, without a laugh, without a look aside, one felt the teeth clenched with rage, the hearts swollen with hatred, a simple resignation to the necessity of the belly.

The nearer Étienne approached the pit the more their number increased. They nearly all walked alone; those who came in groups were in single file, already exhausted, tired of one another and of themselves. He noticed one who was very old, with eyes that shone like hot coals beneath his livid forehead. Another, a young man, was panting with the restrained fury of a storm. Many had their sabots in their hands; one could scarcely hear the soft sound of their coarse woollen stockings on the ground. It was an endless rustling, a general downfall, the forced march of a beaten army, moving on with lowered heads, sullenly absorbed in the desire to renew the struggle and achieve revenge.

When Étienne arrived, Jean-Bart was emerging from the shade; the lanterns, hooked on to the platform, were still burning in the growing dawn. Above the obscure buildings a trail of steam arose like a white plume delicately tinted with carmine. He passed up the sifting-staircase to go to the receiving-room.

The descent was beginning, and the men were coming from the shed. For a moment he stood by, motionless amid the noise and movement. The rolling of the trams shook the metal floor, the drums were turning, unrolling the cables in the midst of cries from the trumpet, the ringing of bells, blows of the mallet on the signal block; he found the monster again swallowing his daily ration of human flesh, the cages rising and plunging, engulfing their burden of men, without ceasing, with the facile gulp of a voracious giant. Since his accident he had a nervous horror of the mine. The cages, as they sank down, tore his bowels. He had to turn away his head; the pit exasperated him.

But in the vast and still sombre hall, feebly lighted up by the exhausted lanterns, he could perceive no friendly face. The miners, who were waiting there with bare feet and their lamps in their hands, looked at him with large restless eyes, and then lowered their faces, drawing back with an air of shame. No doubt they knew him and no longer had any spite against him; they seemed, on the contrary, to fear him, blushing at the thought that he would reproach them with cowardice. This attitude made his heart swell; he forgot that these wretches had stoned him, he again began to dream or changing them into heroes, of directing a whole people, this force of nature which was devouring itself. A cage was embarking its men, and the batch disappeared; as others arrived he saw at last one of his lieutenants in the strike, a worthy fellow who had sworn to die.

"You too!" he murmured, with aching heart.

The other turned pale and his lips trembled; then, with a movement of excuse:

"What would you have? I've got a wife."

Now in the new crowd coming from the shed he recognized them all.

"You too! – you too! – you too!"

And all shrank back, stammering in choked voices:

"I have a mother." – "I have children." – "One must get bread."

The cage did not reappear; they waited for it mournfully, with such sorrow at their defeat that they avoided meeting each other's eyes, obstinately gazing at the shaft.

"And Maheude?" Étienne asked.

They made no reply. One made a sign that she was coming. Others raised their arms, trembling with pity. Ah, poor woman! what wretchedness! The silence continued, and when Étienne stretched out his hand to bid them farewell, they all pressed it vigorously, putting into that mute squeeze their rage at having yielded, their feverish hope of revenge. The cage was there; they got into it and sank, devoured by the gulf.

Pierron had appeared with his naked captain's lamp fixed into the leather of his cap. For the past week he had been chief of the gang at the pit-eye, and the men moved away, for promotion had rendered him bossy. The sight of Étienne annoyed him; he came up, however, and was at last reassured when the young man announced his departure. They talked. His wife now kept the Estaminet du Progrés, thanks to the support of all those gentlemen, who had been so good to her. But he interrupted himself and turned furiously on to Father Mouque, whom he accused of not sending up the dung-heap from his stable at the regulation hour. The old man listened with bent shoulders. Then, before going down, suffering from this reprimand, he, too, gave his hand to Étienne, with the same long pressure as the others, warm with restrained anger and quivering with future rebellion. And this old hand which trembled in his, this old man who was forgiving him for the loss of his dead children, affected Étienne to such a degree that he watched him disappear without saying a word.

"Then Maheude is not coming this morning?" he asked Pierron after a time.

At first the latter pretended not to understand, for there was ill luck even in speaking of her. Then, as he moved away, under the pretext of giving an order, he said at last:

"Eh! Maheude? There she is."

In fact, Maheude had reached the shed with her lamp in her hand, dressed in trousers and jacket, with her head confined in the cap. It was by a charitable exception that the Company, pitying the fate of this unhappy woman, so cruelly afflicted, had allowed her to go down again at the age of forty; and as it seemed difficult to set her again at haulage work, she was employed to manipulate a small ventilator which had been installed in the north gallery, in those infernal regions beneath Tartaret, where there was no movement of air. For ten hours, with aching back, she turned her wheel at the bottom of a burning tube, baked by forty degrees of heat. She earned thirty sous.

When Étienne saw her, a pitiful sight in her male garments – her breast and belly seeming to be swollen by the dampness of the cuttings – he stammered with surprise, trying to find words to explain that he was going away and that he wished to say good-bye to her.

She looked at him without listening, and said at last, speaking familiarly:

"Eh? it surprises you to see me. It's true enough that I threatened to wring the neck of the first of my children who went down again; and now that I'm going down I ought to wring my own, ought I not? Ah, well! I should have done it by now if it hadn't been for the old man and the little ones at the house."

And she went on in her low, fatigued voice. She did not excuse herself, she simply narrated things – that they. had been nearly starved, and that she had made up her mind to it, so that they might not be sent away from the settlement.

"How is the old man?" asked Étienne.

"He is always very gentle and very clean. But he is quite off his nut. He was not brought up for that affair, you know. There was talk of shutting him up with the madmen, but I was not willing; they would have done for him in his soup. His story has, all the same, been very bad for us, for he'll never get his pension; one of those gentlemen told me that it would be immoral to give him one."

"Is Jeanlin working?"

"Yes, those gentlemen found something for him to do at the top. He gets twenty sous. Oh! I don't complain; the bosses have been very good, as they told me themselves. The brat's twenty sous and my thirty, that makes fifty. If there were not six of us we should get enough to eat. Estelle devours now, and the worst is that it will be four or five years before Lénore and Henri are old enough to come to the pit."

Étienne could not restrain a movement of pain.

"They, too!"

Maheude's pale cheeks turned red, and her eyes flamed. But her shoulders sank as if beneath the weight of destiny.

"What would you have? They after the others. They have all been done for there; now it's their turn."

She was silent; some landers, who were rolling trains, disturbed them. Through the large dusty windows the early sun was entering, drowning the lanterns in grey light; and the engine moved every three minutes, the cables unrolled, the cages continued to swallow down men.

"Come along, you loungers, look sharp!" shouted Pierron. "Get in; we shall never have done with it today." Maheude, whom he was looking at, did not stir. She had already allowed three cages to pass, and she said, as though arousing herself and remembering Étienne's first words:

"Then you're going away?"

"Yes, this morning."

"You're right; better be somewhere else if one can. And I'm glad to have seen you, because you can know now, anyhow, that I've nothing on my mind against you. For a moment I could have killed you, after all that slaughter. But one thinks, doesn't one? One sees that when all's reckoned up it's nobody's fault. No, no! it's not your fault; it's the fault of everybody."

Now she talked with tranquillity of her dead, of her man, of Zacharie, of Catherine; and tears only came into her eyes when she uttered Alzire's name. She had resumed her calm reasonableness, and judged things sensibly. It would bring no luck to the middle class to have killed so many poor people. Sure enough, they would be punished for it one day, for everything has to be paid for. There would even be no need to interfere; the whole thing would explode by itself. The soldiers would fire on the masters just as they had fired on the men. And in her everlasting resignation, in that hereditary discipline under which she was again bowing, a conviction had established itself, the certainty that injustice could not last longer, and that, if there were no good God left, another would spring up to avenge the wretched.

She spoke in a low voice, with suspicious glances round. Then, as Pierron was coming up, she added, aloud:

"Well, if you're going, you must take your things from our house. There are still two shirts, three handkerchiefs, and an old pair of trousers."

Étienne, with a gesture, refused these few things saved from the dealers.

"No, it's not worth while; they can be for the children. At Paris I can arrange for myself."

Two more cages had gone down, and Pierron decided to speak straight to Maheude.

"I say now, over there, they are waiting for you! Is that little chat nearly done?"

But she turned her back. Why should he be so zealous, this man who had sold himself? The descent didn't concern him. His men hated him enough already on his level. And she persisted, with her lamp in her hand, frozen amid the draughts in spite of the mildness of the season. Neither Étienne nor she found anything more to say. They remained facing each other with hearts so full that they would have liked to speak once more.

At last she spoke for the sake of speaking.

"The Levaque is in the family way. Levaque is still in prison; Bouteloup is taking his place meanwhile."

"Ah, yes! Bouteloup."

"And, listen! did I tell you? Philoméne has gone away."

"What! gone away?"

"Yes, gone away with a Pas-de-Calais miner. I was afraid she would leave the two brats on me. But no, she took them with her. Eh? A woman who spits blood and always looks as if she were on the point of death!"

She mused for a moment, and then went on in a slow voice:

"There's been talk on my account. You remember they said I slept with you. Lord! After my man's death that might very well have happened if I had been younger. But now I'm glad it wasn't so, for we should have regretted it, sure enough."

"Yes, we should have regretted it," Étienne repeated, simply.

That was all; they spoke no more. A cage was waiting for her; she was being called angrily, threatened with a fine. Then she made up her mind, and pressed his hand. Deeply moved, he still looked at her, so worn and worked out, with her livid face, her discoloured hair escaping from the blue cap, her body as of a good over-fruitful beast, deformed beneath the jacket and trousers. And in this last pressure of the hands he felt again the long, silent pressure of his mates, giving him a rendezvous for the day when they would begin again. He understood perfectly. There was a tranquil faith in the depths of her eyes. It would be soon, and this time it would be the final blow.

"What a damned shammer!" exclaimed Pierron.

Pushed and hustled, Maheude squeezed into a tram with four others. The signal-cord was drawn to strike for meat, the cage was unhooked and fell into the night, and there was nothing more but the rapid flight of the cable.

Then Étienne left the pit. Below, beneath the screening-shed, he noticed a creature seated on the earth, with legs stretched out, in the midst of a thick pile of coal. It was Jeanlin, who was employed there to clean the large coal. He held a block of coal between his thighs, and freed it with a hammer from the fragments of slate. A fine powder drowned him in such a flood of soot that the young man would never have recognized him if the child had not lifted his ape-like face, with the protruding ears and small greenish eyes. He laughed, with a joking air, and, giving a final blow to the block, disappeared in the black dust which arose.

Outside, Étienne followed the road for a while, absorbed in his thoughts. All sorts of ideas were buzzing in his head. But he felt the open air, the free sky, and he breathed deeply. The sun was appearing in glory at the horizon, there was a reawakening of gladness over the whole country. A flood of gold rolled from the east to the west on the immense plain. This heat of life was expanding and extending in a tremor of youth, in which vibrated the sighs of the earth, the song of birds, all the murmuring sounds of the waters and the woods. It was good to live, and the old world wanted to live through one more spring.

And penetrated by that hope, Étienne slackened his walk, his eyes wandering to right and to left amid the gaiety of the new season. He thought about himself, he felt himself strong, seasoned by his hard experiences at the bottom of the mine. His education was complete, he was going away armed, a rational soldier of the revolution, having declared war against society as he saw it and as he condemned it. The joy of rejoining Pluchart and of being, like Pluchart, a leader who was listened to, inspired him with speeches, and he began to arrange the phrases. He was meditating an enlarged programme; that middle-class refinement, which had raised him above his class, had deepened his hatred of the middle class. He felt the need of glorifying these workers, whose odour of wretchedness was now unpleasant to him; he would show that they alone were great and stainless, the only nobility and the only strength in which humanity could be dipped afresh. He already saw himself in the tribune, triumphing with the people, if the people did not devour him.

The loud song of a lark made him look up towards the sky. Little red clouds, the last vapours of the night, were melting in the limpid blue; and the vague faces of Souvarine and Rasseneur came to his memory. Decidedly, all was spoilt when each man tried to get power for himself. Thus that famous International which was to have renewed the world had impotently miscarried, and its formidable army had been cut up and crumbled away from internal dissensions. Was Darwin right, then, and the world only a battlefield, where the strong ate the weak for the sake of the beauty and continuance of the race? This question troubled him, although he settled it like a man who is satisfied with his knowledge. But one idea dissipated his doubts and enchanted him

– that of taking up his old explanation of the theory the first time that he should speak. If any class must be devoured, would not the people, still new and full of life, devour the middle class, exhausted by enjoyment? The new society would arise from new blood. And in this expectation of an invasion of barbarians, regenerating the old decayed nations, reappeared his absolute faith in an approaching revolution, the real one – that of the workers – the fire of which would inflame this century's end with that purple of the rising sun which he saw like blood on the sky. He still walked, dreaming, striking his dog-wood stick against the flints on the road, and when he glanced around him he recognized the various places. Just there, at the Fourche-aux-Boeufs, he remembered that he had taken command of the band that morning when the pits were sacked. Today the brutish, deathly, ill-paid work was beginning over again. Beneath the earth, down there at seven hundred metres, it seemed to him he heard low, regular, continuous blows; it was the men he had just seen go down, the black workers, who were hammering in their silent rage. No doubt they were beaten. They had left their dead and their money on the field; but Paris would not forget the volleys fired at the Voreux, and the blood of the empire, too, would flow from that incurable wound. And if the industrial crisis was drawing to an end, if the workshops were opening again one by one, a state of war was no less declared, and peace was henceforth impossible. The colliers had reckoned up their men; they had tried their strength, with their cry for justice arousing the workers all over France. Their defeat, therefore, reassured no one. The Montsou bourgeois, in their victory, felt the vague uneasiness that arses on the morrow of a strike, looking behind them to see if their end did not lie inevitably over there, in spite of all beyond that great silence. They understood that the revolution would be born again unceasingly, perhaps tomorrow, with a general strike – the common understanding of all workers having general funds, and so able to hold out for months, eating their own bread. This time push only had been given to a ruinous society, but they had heard the rumbling beneath their feet, and they felt more shocks arising, and still more, until the old edifice would be crushed, fallen in and swallowed, going down like the Voreux to the abyss.

Étienne took the Joiselle road, to the left. He remembered that he had prevented the band from rushing on to Gaston-Marie. Afar, in the clear sky he saw the steeples of several pits – Mirou to the right, Madeleine and Crévecoeur side by side. Work was going on everywhere; he seemed to be able to catch the blows of the pick at the bottom of the earth, striking now from one end of the plain to the other, one blow, and another blow, and yet more blows, beneath the fields and roads and villages which were laughing in the light, all the obscure labour of the underground prison, so crushed by the enormous mass of the rocks that one had to know it was underneath there to distinguish its great painful sigh. And he now thought that, perhaps, violence would not hasten things. Cutting cables, tearing up rails, breaking lamps. what a useless task it was! It was not worth while for three thousand men to rush about in a devastating band doing that. He vaguely divined that lawful methods might one day be more terrible. His reason was ripening, he had sown the wild oats of his spite. Yes, Maheude had well said, with her good sense, that that would be the great blow — to organize quietly, to know one another, to unite in associations when the laws would permit it; then, on the morning when they felt their strength, and millions of workers would be face to face with a few thousand idlers, to take the power into their own hands and become the masters. Ah! what a reawakening of truth and justice! The sated and crouching god would at once get his death-blow, the monstrous idol hidden in the depths of his sanctuary, in that unknown distance where poor wretches fed him with their flesh without ever having seen him.

But Étienne, leaving the Vandame road, now came on to the paved street. On the right he saw Montsou, which was lost in the valley. Opposite were the ruins of the

Voreux, the accursed hole where three pumps worked unceasingly. Then there were the other pits at the horizon, the Victoire, Saint-Thomas, Feutry-Cantel; while, towards the north, the tall chimneys of the blast furnaces, and the batteries of coke ovens, were smoking in the transparent morning air. If he was not to lose the eight o'clock train he must hasten, for he had still six kilometres before him.

And beneath his feet, the deep blows, those obstinate blows of the pick, continued. The mates were all there; he heard them following him at every stride. Was not that Maheude beneath the beetroots. with bent back and hoarse respiration accompanying the rumble of the ventilator? To left, to right, farther on, he seemed to recognize others beneath the wheatfields, the hedges, the young trees. Now the April sun, in the open sky, was shining in his glory, and warming the pregnant earth. From its fertile flanks life was leaping out, buds were bursting into green leaves, and the fields were quivering with the growth of the grass. On every side seeds were swelling, stretching out, cracking the plain, filled by the need of heat and light. An overflow of sap was mixed with whispering voices, the sound of the germs expanding in a great kiss. Again and again, more and more distinctly, as though they were approaching the soil, the mates were hammering. In the fiery rays of the sun on this youthful morning the country seemed full of that sound. Men were springing forth, a black avenging army, germinating slowly in the furrows, growing towards the harvests of the next century, and their germination would soon overturn the earth.

www.ReadHowYouWant.com

You can buy our **Large Type** and **EasyRead** books from our www.ReadHowYouWant.com website, from websites like Amazon.com and through your UK and North American bookshop.

EasyRead books are designed to make your reading easy and enjoyable. **EasyRead** books are published in different font sizes, so you can select the font size best for you.

EasyRead is for people with normal eyesight who want books in an easy-to-read format.

EasyRead Comfort is for people who find reading small print tiring but do not need large print.

EasyRead Large is for people who find it easier to read larger print.

The **EasyRead** font, character, word and line spacing have all been set to make it as easy as possible both to recognize a word, and to run your eye along a line of text without losing your place. We split as few words as possible at line ends, as split words make reading harder and can be annoying. For out-of-copyright books, words have been changed to modern spelling (where the sense is not affected), and the original hyphenation of compound words has been retained where this improves word recognition or sense.

With most things you buy, you get a choice, and you can choose the make and model that suits best. There is a big exception – books. You don't get to choose a format that is easy for you to read – you have to read the format the publisher selects.

This "**One Size Fits All**" paradigm **no longer** need apply to books.

At www.ReadHowYouWant.com, you can order a book just as you want it, so you can read it easily. You can choose nearly any format, and at a surprisingly low cost, because of a technical breakthrough that allows us to typeset an individual book automatically, print and bind the book and have it quickly sent directly to you.

You can have your book in **Talking Book** formats (**DAISY or MP3**) or as an **E-book** or in **Braille**.

We have developed totally new visual formats which we hope will help people with **dyslexia** and other print reading disabilities. Look at www.ReadHowYouWant.com for more information.

Good news for publishers and authors. There is a big market for large type, personalized and accessible format books. We can help publishers and authors find new market opportunities for their books, and selling your book through www.ReadHowY ouWant.com is easy – we do the work for you. Contact us on info@ReadHowYouWant .com.

Printed in the United States
69030LVS00001B/85